VOSS

VOSS

How I Come to America and Am Hero, Mostly

DAVID IVES

G. P. Putnam's Sons

G. P. PUTNAM'S SONS
A division of Penguin Young Readers Group.
Published by The Penguin Group.
Penguin Group (USA) Inc., 375 Hudson Street, New York, NY 10014, U.S.A. Penguin Group (Canada), 90 Eglinton Avenue East, Suite 700, Toronto, Ontario M4P 2Y3, Canada (a division of Pearson Penguin Canada Inc.). Penguin Books Ltd, 80 Strand, London WC2R 0RL, England. Penguin Ireland, 25 St. Stephen's Green, Dublin 2, Ireland (a division of Penguin Books Ltd). Penguin Group (Australia), 250 Camberwell Road, Camberwell, Victoria 3124, Australia (a division of Pearson Australia Group Pty Ltd). Penguin Books India Pvt Ltd, 11 Community Centre, Panchsheel Park, New Delhi—110 017, India. Penguin Group (NZ), 67 Apollo Drive, Rosedale, North Shore 0632, New Zealand (a division of Pearson New Zealand Ltd). Penguin Books (South Africa) (Pty) Ltd, 24 Sturdee Avenue, Rosebank, Johannesburg 2196, South Africa. Penguin Books Ltd, Registered Offices: 80 Strand, London WC2R 0RL, England.

Printed in the United States of America.
Design by Richard Amari.
Text set in Mendoza Roman.

Library of Congress Cataloging-in-Publication Data
Ives, David. Voss / David Ives. p. cm. Summary: Through a series of letters home, fifteen-year-old Vospop "Voss" Vsklzwczdztwczky shares his experiences as he is smuggled out of Slobovia in a crate of black-market cheese puffs, tries to find a job in an American city, and foils a sinister plot. [1. Illegal aliens—Fiction. 2. Emigration and immigration—Fiction. 3. Donation of organs, tissues, etc.—Fiction. 4. Letters—Fiction. 5. Humorous stories.] I. Title. PZ7 I1948Vos 2008 [Fic]—dc22 2007046207
ISBN 978-0-399-24722-4 10 9 8 7 6 5 4 3 2 1

I pity the poor immigrant
who wishes he would've stayed home.

—*Bob Dylan*
  "I Pity the Poor Immigrant"

Leave and learn.

—*Old Slobovian saying*

Hello!

Or, as we say in Slobovian, Bushweck!

Perhaps you have read about me in your newspeepers. Perhaps you have seen my peekture on your front pages. If so, you know that I am a 15-year-old illegal immigrunt Slobovian boy who got into dipp, dipp trobble.

My name: Vospop Vsklzwczdztwczky. This is a name nobody can forget, because nobody can pronounce it. Donut try to pronounce me. You will only hurt yourself! In ancient Slobovian, my name means "car crash." It also sounds like car crash. So, plizz, call me Voss. A good, easy, American-sounding name!

You will learn all my American experiences in the ladders I wrote to my good friend Meero. In these ladders you will also learn about my gloomy father, Bogdown, and my crazy Uncle Shpoont and the dipp, dipp trobble I got into.

Maybe from my ladders you will learn what to do. Maybe you will learn what not to do. Or maybe not? In any cases, donut do what I did. As pipple say in Slobovia: Be yourself, mostly.

Welcome to my experiences!

Vospop

LADDER ONE
How My Uncle Shpoont Went Crazy and Decided to Go to America

May 1st
Aboard sheep

To Meero Mrkz
At the House with the Red Fence
and the Yellow Outhouse
Stoppova, Slobovia, 90211-000000

Bushweck, Meero!

You won't believe this, my friend.

We made it out of Slobovia! We are bound for America! We have smoggled ourselves aboard a great big sheep, the cargo freighter SSS *Windmill*.

And Meero, we are headed for dipp, dipp trobble.

I write you this ladder from inside a steel freight container. We are somewhere in the meedle of the Atlantical Ocean. It could be day outside, it could be night. Inside this freight container are me, my father Bogdown, and my Uncle Shpoont— plus one hundred thousand packits of blackmarket imitation Cheez Puffs.

I have never been on a transatlantical sheep before.

My advice? Donut do it, Meero!

The sheep goes up. My insides go down. The sheep goes down. My insides go up. The sheep rolls to one side and I feel how small I am. I take our ancient family pocket watch from my pocket and look at the time, hoping it will be America soon. The sheep rolls again . . .

I am no brave boy, Meero, as you know. I am what is called in Eenglish a "worry wart." This is what we call in Slobovian a *furri fart*. America has no place for *furri farts*!

I do not write you in Slobovian because I want to practice my Eenglishes. This way in America, I will not sound like eediot. The deefeecold thing about the Eenglish linguitch is the articles. By articles I mean these words *a, an,* and *the.* Very misterious words, these articles! What is the difference, Meero, between "*a* dog," "*the* dog," and "*an* dog"?

These articles are hard to master because the Slobovian linguitch has no articles. Slobovian pipple are too poor to have articles. We donut say, "The dog chased the squirrel." We say, "Dog chased squirrel." We donut say, "The toilet exploded." We say, "Toilet exploded." Most often we say, "Toilet exploded *again.*"

But let me tell you, Meero, how the dipp, dipp trobble began. You won't believe me, mostly!

When last I saw you last, you and I were shaking hands and embracing and saying goodbye in Stoppova, our *eetski-beetski* village in Lower Slobovia. I had my suitcase beside me. You had George Clooney, your cow.

How we wept, Meero, tinking we might never meet again! I wiped my eyes on my gray fedora hat. You wiped your eyes on George. The morning light made a million mirrors of the puddles in the mud. Maybe in America, I will meet the real George Clooney, for whom you named your cow. I will say hello from you, Meero! I will tell him he is named for cow in Slobovia!

(You must forgive me my liking for exaggeration points at the ends of my sentences. I am seemply an excitable boy!)

Do you remember that morning, Meero? How my father Bogdown and my Uncle Shpoont came down the road with their suitcases? My father Bogdown trudged as if his suitcase was loaded with rocks instead of two clean white shirts and seven pairs of clean underwares and nothing elses. My Uncle Shpoont strolled along as if he owned the world. He beamed, as always. He also floffed his magnificent mustache to let some sunlight amongst the dense, dark bristles. His handlebar eyebrows waggled with joy.

The two men were dressed exactly like you and me. They were dressed as all Slobovian men dress, in buttoned blue suits and clean white shirts and black stringy ties and our polished black shoes with shoelaces. All of us wore Slobovian national symbol, the bowling pin, in our lapels.

"Come, Vospop!" my uncle called. "America awaits us! I want to see my new country!"

Your twin cousins, Lilka and Lilka, ran out of their house. They were dressed in those flowered Slobovian dresses that look like they are made from peeg iron. They also wore those square shoes that look like they are still in the shoe box. Perhaps someday you and Lilka and Lilka will want to come to

America. Maybe George Clooney, too. There must be room for you. Is very big country, America!

(Is very small, Slobovia!)

Lilka and Lilka gave us some of their famous Stoppova pop-overs for the journey, still warm from the oven. They then embraced my father Bogdown and wished him a safe voyage.

"America will be wonderful!" Lilka said.

"America will be beautiful!" Lilka said.

My father shrogged and quoted the old Slobovian proverb: *"Don't count your chickens. You don't have any."*

As you know, when my mother died, my father lost all por-poise in life and fell into deep-pression. He has taken to quot-ing old Slobovian proverbs. He likes the most gloomy ones. For example: *Today is the first day of somebody else's life.* Here is another of his favorites: *It is always darkest before the dawn, except maybe tomorrow.*

Though my father Bogdown has grown gloomy, he is still strong. He is, of course, the undefeated Tree-Throwing Cham-pion of Lower Slobovia. You remember him in the annual tree-throwing competition on Saint Slobovius Day? Oak trees, pine trees, redwood trees, shoe trees, Christmas trees, even family trees. You name it, he threw it. But after my dear mother died, my father lost his taste for throwing trees. He quotes gloomy proverbs instead.

Having embraced my gloomy father, Lilka and Lilka em-braced my uncle.

Lilka said to him, "Can you believe it?"

Lilka said, "To America?"

"America?" my uncle roared to the empty street. "*I OWN IT!*"

As you know, my uncle has always been unusual. As young man he wanted to be great Shiksepeerean actor—what we in Slobovia call a *shmackter*. (Such beautiful word!) He did become the greatest shmackter in Slobovia, but only because he was *only* shmackter in Slobovia. This was great career. He had to do nothing!

Now he has this crazy idea that he owns everything. This comes from watching too much the commercials on American television. When my uncle calls Stoppova "my village," he does not mean "my village." He means "*my* village." He thinks he owns the fields, the houses, the churches, the grass, the trees, everything for as far as you could see. You can name anything in the world and my uncle thinks he owns it. This includes also the Great Wall of China and all of Disneyland and Australia.

Who can tell him no? Who will remind him that actually he owns nothing?

Do you know the story, Meero? I went to my uncle's house one day to bring him a slice of fresh-baked horseradish pie. He was, of course, watching American television. Indeed, he was watching the 24-Hour American Commercial Channel. He stared at screen like heepnotized person. The screen was fool of glowing objects for sale. The glowing objects were mirrored in my uncle's bulging eyes.

"Vospop," my uncle said, "we must go to America."

"For what porpoise, Uncle?" I asked him.

"So that I may view my American properties, of course!" He pointed at screen. "You see everything I own?"

This is what comes of watching American commercials twenty-four hours a day, Meero. You get washbrained!

"How will we get to America, Uncle?" I asked him.

"Maybe we will smoggle ourselves. Maybe we will take one of my airplanes. That's the whole secret about the world," my uncle told me. "You gotta *tink*, Vospop."

"I tink I tink too much already, Uncle."

"Nobody," said my uncle, "can tink too much."

Trobbled by this, I went to see my father Bogdown at Shamus Onyoosky's wood-shaving factory.

My father stood at his workbench, slicing wood shavings off a 75-foot tree. He had shaved the tree down to a perfect, smooth, 75-foot plank, one eench thick. My father Bogdown would keep shaving the plank till it was a half eench thick, then a quarter eench thick, then one sixteenth of eench, then only one shave thick. He would shave it until it disappeared under his hand and turned into air.

"Poppup," I said, "Uncle Shpoont tinks he owns everything and wants to go to America."

My father merely quoted the old Slobovian saying, *"Nothing ventured, nobody blamed."* This meant No.

Two months later, Shamus Onyoosky had to close down his wood-shaving factory. The bottom had fallen out of the world wood-shavings market. Stoppova was no longer Woodshaver To The World. My father was out of job.

One day, having his usual beer and cornflakes for breakfast, my father said, "We are leaving for America."

And so we left.

My hand is cramping, Meero. Tomorrow I will tell you about this dipp, dipp trobble we have gotten ourselves into!

Your eternal friend,

Vospop

LADDER TWO
How We Hitched a Ride to America and Started All the Trobble

Bushweck, Meero!

So there we were, standing before your house, departing for America. You will remember how Uncle Shpoont embraced Lilka and bounced her up and down a few times. He then embraced Lilka and bounced her up and down a few times.

"Good Slobovian women!" he cried as he bounced. "Built like fire hydrants! Be prosperous! Be virtuous! Be clean!"

Then, you remember, he snepped open his coin purse. He took out three old buttons and gave one button to you and one to Lilka and one to Lilka.

"Treat yourselves," Uncle Shpoont said. "It's on me!"

"Those are buttons, Shpoont," my father growled.

"They are tokens of inestimable value, Bogdown," my uncle said. "And *there's more where that came from!*"

"Goodbye, Vospop," you said to me in Eenglish. Tears puddled in your eyes. Then you could not resist repeating in Slobovian. "*Beckwash,* Vospop!" And at that, the tears rolled down your chicks.

Leaving you and Lilka and Lilka and George Clooney, we walked up the road through town. At our backs we heard you and Lilka and Lilka calling out your fading farewells.

"Beckwash . . . ! Beckwash . . . ! Beckwash . . . !"

Ah, Meero, I began to be homeseek already. We passed the Church of Saint Hernia, where I celebrated my First Holy Accordion. We passed the field where my father, in happier days, threw trees at the Saint Slobovius Day Fair. We passed the house where my uncle's goddaughter, Leena Aleenska, used to live. It has been boarded up now for three years, since Leena Aleenska and Grandma Aleenska smoggled themselves to America in a crate filled with jars of home-dilled peekles.

Beyond the village, at the top of the hill, I turned and looked back over Stoppova. My uncle looked back, too. His hand pressed my shoulder.

"Don't worry, Vospop," he said. "There's more world where that came from."

For two whole days we walked toward America. What else could we do without train fare? My father had perhaps 50 Slobovian *slotkeys* in his pocket. My uncle had a coin purse full of old buttons. I had nothing at all. I had, as we say in Slobovian, *neetchi.*

By nightfall of the second day, I was exhausted.

We were walking in a muddy ditch beside a road. "Uncle," I said, "are we going to have to walk all the way to America? *You* own all this. Do something!"

I was peevish, Meero. And peevishness is a great evil! As you know, peevishness is one of the Twelve Pretty Big Sins. The others are whining, carping, barking, moping, nose-picking, nose-picking-and-flicking-your-snot-into-the-air-instead-of-a-handkerchief, buttox-pinching, telling a joke badly, popping your chewing gum, whistling without a tune, and urinating outside the bowl without wiping it up.

Uncle Shpoont looked at me as if I had brought him back to his senses.

"Vospop," my uncle said, "you are right. What am I tinking?"

We heard the roar of a big truck approaching.

He handed me his suitcase. "Hold this," he said.

He climbed up from the ditch and stepped into the meedle of the road! Meero, he walked straight into the path of great big truck barreling our way.

Uncle Shpoont held up a hand in front of himself.

"*Stop,*" he said calmly.

A crash of gears. A squeal of brakes. A string of shouted curses from the truck driver. The truck screeched to a halt only eenches from my uncle.

The truck driver banged out of the cab, cursing my uncle, who remained calm in meedle of the road. What the obseenity are you doing, the truck driver shouted, get the obseenity out of the obseenity road, do you obseenity want to be killed, et cetera and so forth.

My uncle waited until the truck driver was out of obseenities.

"What are you doing with my truck?" asked Uncle Shpoont.

"*Your* truck?" the driver said. "This is not *your* truck. This is *Bilias Opchuck's* truck. You know Bilias Opchuck?"

The driver wore a leather cap so greasy you could have lit a match and used him for a candle. He took off this greasy cap and wrung it in his hands, as pipple do when speaking of Bilias Opchuck.

"Of course I know him!" my uncle said. "Who does not know Bilias Opchuck? Imitation blackmarketeer and smoggler."

"Also," the truck driver added, *"assassin."*

My uncle said: "He works for me."

The truck driver was astoundished. "Bilias Opchuck works for *you?*" he cried. "Are you obseenity joking?"

Of course, nobody would ever joke about Bilias Opchuck. Nobody would say he was Bilias Opchuck's boss. Bilias Opchuck would keel him, mostly. Bilias Opchuck was such a devoted criminal, he only ate crimini mushrooms. He was such a thief that for desserts, he ate only the cakes that Germans call *stollen*. The stollen were, of course, stolen stollen. A man once stole a look at Bilias Opchuck in a tavern. Bilias Opchuck traveled fifty miles to steal it back.

"Why are you using such obseenities to me?" my uncle said.

"I'm sorry," truck driver stammered.

Uncle Shpoont pointed to the steel freight container loaded on the back of the truck.

"What are you transporting, driver?" he asked.

"One million packits of imitation blackmarket Cheez Puffs," truck driver said. "These are Bilias Opchuck's Cheez Puffs, bound for Moscow."

"Wrong!" my uncle corrected him. "These Cheez Puffs belong to *me* and you are transporting us to America. Open this."

He tapped on the door to the steel container and called to my father.

"Bogdown! Come out of ditch! My truck is taking us to America!"

The truck driver kissed my uncle's hand and opened a door in the steel container. My uncle gazed with satisfaction upon his million imitation plastic packits of imitation blackmarket Cheez Puffs.

"I will not punish you," my uncle said to the truck driver. "But donut do it again."

The driver bowed as we climbed up into the container. Uncle Shpoont arranged a heap of Cheez Puffs into a kind of sofa. Meanwhile, my father Bogdown trudged up from the ditch and joined us inside the freight container without a word.

"You have done well, driver," my uncle said. "I will bang on the side when we need some urination. Carry on."

"Thank you, sir! Thank you!" cried the truck driver.

He closed the door of the steel container. A moment later, the truck lurched, and we were on our way.

"Well, Bogdown," my uncle said. He clapped my father on the back. "America!"

"Uncle Shpoont," I said, "you donut tink we'll get into trobble? Hijacking a shipment of Bilias Opchuck's imitation blackmarket Cheez Puffs? And taking them to America instead of Moscow?"

"First of all," my uncle reasoned, "they are *my* imitation blackmarket Cheez Puffs. Second, *donut worry*."

Two days later we got loaded from truck onto the SSS *Windmill*. By now my hair was orange from itting too many imitation blackmarket Cheez Puffs. Also, my head glowed in the dark. But a glowing head is not dipp trobble.

Stealing one million imitation blackmarket Cheez Puffs from Bilias Opchuck?

This is trobble. This is dipp, *dipp* trobble, Meero. For Bilias Opchuck forgets nothing and he forgives nothing. He will find us sometime and ask for his Cheez Puffs back. I donut want to be there when he does.

To be continued!

Your friend even more eternal
than before but worried,

Vospop

LADDER THREE
We Arrive in America

Dear (*as we say in America*) Meero!

So there we were, deep in the sheep. I donut know how many days we tossed over the bottomless Atlantical Ocean in our freight container. (Or should I say, in our *afraid* container?) Then one day we heard a distant cry.

"*Land ho!*"

My uncle and I sat up as if electrified. We could not believe each other's ears. The cry came again.

"*LAND HO!*"

I could not resist, Meero. Even though someone might catch me, I flung open the door of the freight container. I ran across the wet and sleepery deck to the rail of the sheep. My uncle joined me there.

At first I saw nothing. Then I detected a razor-thin wire of land betwin the blue sea and the blue sky. Balanced on that wire like a rope dancer stood a great, shining city. I only wished I knew which city it was! It could have been New York City, New York. It could have been San Francisco, Arizona. It could have been Detritus, Michigan.

America, Meero!

"How do you like America?" Uncle Shpoont said.

"I like it so far, Uncle Shpoont," I said. "I like it very much."

"Good!" he said. "Someday it will be yours. I will leave it to you in my will."

My father Bogdown came up beside us at the rail and stared without interest at the horizon.

"Look, Poppup," I said. "America!"

He speet over the rail and muttered another old, old proverb. *"Let's cross that bridge before it falls in the river."*

I did not know what this means. No doubt it was gloomy.

We returned to our freight container. Sometime later, we felt a *bump* as the sheep came to dock. Later after that, we heard something clang against the top of the container and the shouts of men outside. Then the floor of the freight container tipped this way and that, and we all fell over.

The container was being flown through the air on cables, Meero! We scrambled about the floor for balance as we continued to tip and padded ourselves with Cheez Puffs.

Then the container went *bump* again, and the tipping stopped. We rose cautiously and found solid ground under our feet. We had been set on land.

I opened the door and there was America outside! In fool color!

My uncle said, "Wait here, Vospop, while I go find a customer."

He disappeared down the row of containers on the dock.

Men ran by, paying me no attention. I gazed upon the rusty sheep that had carried us across the vastnesses of the ocean. Such a fragile vessel to have carried us so many thousands of miles!

A short while later, my uncle returned with a sweaty man in a peeling bleck leather jacket. The man had a soft, sagging face, as if he was melting.

"I understand you got a lotta *Cheez Puffs* you wanna un-load?" the sagging man said. He had a voice like dirty water at the bottom of gurgling toilet.

My uncle led him inside the freight container and showed him the one million packits of imitation blackmarket Cheez Puffs.

"How much?" the saggy man gurgled.

"One hundred thousand dollars," my uncle said.

The man did not seem surprised by the price. He took a packit of Cheez Puffs and studied it. As he did so, he fished in his nose and pulled out a clump of nostril hairs. Then he snizzed.

"Hey, wait a minute. What's this?" he said. He fleeked the nostril hair away and read from the packit. *"Chiss Poffs?"*

"Of course!" my uncle said. "Cheez Puffs!"

"It don't say Cheez Puffs here. It says *Chiss Poffs.*"

"The Slobovian spelling," my uncle said.

The saggy man read onward. *"You lick Chiss Poffs.* What's that supposed to mean?"

"You will like Cheez Puffs," my uncle translated.

"Yeah, but it says, *You lick Chiss Poffs.*"

"Small Slobovian typing error," my uncle said.

The man read on. "*You lick Chiss Poffs. Very hellty and good for one. Ploss, tasty!* Who's gonna buy this?"

He squeezed the packit.

"It's crumbs!" he said. He took up another packit and another. "They're *all* crumbs!"

"Well," my uncle said reasonably, "we have been leaving on them. They are yours for one hundred thousand American dollars."

The man snepped out a bill from his wallet. "I'll give you twenty bucks for the lot."

"I take it," said my uncle.

We left the Chiss Poffs to Mr. Gurgly Toilet Voice, took up our suitcases, and walked out of the dockyard. We had proved the old Slobovian saying, Meero. *Crumbs do not pay.*

As we headed through the dockyard gate, a shiny black Nogo sedan came roaring down the street. We had to flatten ourselves against the dockyard gate to let it go by. It raced at full speed—straight toward where the SSS *Windmill* was docked.

The Nogo is of course the Slobovian national car. Only a Slobovian would drive a Nogo. Only a Slobovian *could* drive a Nogo. And only one parteecular Slobovian would be driving his Nogo into this parteecular dockyard on this parteecular day.

Bilias Opchuck.

I could see Bilias Opchuck's ham-shaped head in the back as the car swerved by us. He wanted his Chiss Poffs. Or he wanted Uncle Shpoont. Or he wanted his money.

Uncle Shpoont did not seem to notice the Nogo. He strolled out the dockyard gate as ever, as if he owned the world.

Evening was starting to fall as we entered our first city street. It was lined with car dealers, fist food joints, bail bond offices, and pornographical shops. As you know, Meero, Slobovia has no pornographs. All these naked pipples, they have nothing better to do? Poot some clothes on, naked pipples, and find a job! Read book! Uncover cure for cancer! You can do nothing naked but waste your time!

"Uncle Shpoont," I said, "where are we going?"

"Where there is life, Vospop," said Uncle Shpoont, "there are Slobovians. We only need to find them! Besides, I have twenty American dollars. Onward!"

Pipple stared at us and pointed. We must have looked most interesting, two men and a boy in gray fedora hats and blue suits and white shirts and stringy ties and polished black shoes with shoelaces. Americans do not wear such things. Americans dress like they are going to the bitch for suntan. Many pipple here wear in the street those rubber bitch sandals that in Slobovia we only wear in the shower. They call them "fleep-flops" here.

We passed more car dealers, more fist food shops, more bail bond offices, and many more pornographical shops. Then my uncle spotted an empty yellow taxicab.

"Good evening hello!" my uncle called out. *"Meester Taxi!"*

The taxicab driver stopped and looked out his taxi window at our gray fedora hats and blue suits. He was a brown man, and he wore a beautiful white turban like a giant meringue on his head. It spiraled over his face as if pure thoughts were swirling out of his brains.

"Very tasteful national dress," he said in a lilting, melodic exsent. "*Ohmygodyes!*"

My uncle said, "You know where we can find horseradish pie?"

"Horseradish pie?" the driver said. "*Ohmygodyes!* In the illegal Slobovian part of town."

"Why is it called the *illegal* Slobovian part?" I asked.

"Because all the Slobovians there," the cabdriver said, "are illegal. *Ohmygodyes.*"

"Take us to the illegal Slobovian section!" cried Uncle Shpoont.

Our taxicab driver's name was Mr. Awakan Singh, taxi number CO1935. He drove very kveekly, Meero! 50, 60, 70 miles per hour is normal for American taxicabs.

Mr. Awakan Singh watched me in the rearview mirror as I pointed and gawked and craned. My uncle watched it all go by, nodding with approval.

"How do you like my buildings, Vospop?" he said. "How do you like my elevated train? How do you like my river?"

It was all new and beautiful to me. Soon the fist food shops and pornographical places gave way to falling-down apartment houses.

"Look, Uncle!" I exclaimed.

A sign in a restaurant window said: Homemade Horseradish Pie. Underneath, the sign listed today's specials: Chicken Soup With Feathers. Spleen With Okra. Live Sauerkraut.

How it made me water to read these Slobovian delicacies! By these treats we knew that we had entered the illegal Slobovian section of city.

"*Stop!*" cried my uncle.

The taxicab stopped so fast, our buttox left the seat.

"Eighteen dollars and 35 cents," said Mr. Awakan Singh.

My uncle gave him a twenty-dollars bill, plus two buttons from his coin purse.

"Beautiful!" said Mr. Awakan Singh, looking at the buttons. "*Ohmygodyes!* Have a wonderful time in America!"

He zoomed away at 90 miles per hour, leaving us on the curb.

The illegal Slobovian section was a very deep-pressing part of town. There was nothing bright. Nothing clean. Nothing Slobovian. Only rundown apartment buildings and a few shabby shops. Young Slobovian men slouched idly in the doorways wearing gray fedora hats and blue suits and black shoes with shoelaces. But the men's hats were crumpled, their suits wrinkled, their shoes not polished. Why were they not working? Since when do Slobovians do nothing? And since when do they stand apart from each other? Slobovians do not stand apart. They stand togather! They talk, they laugh, they take out their accordions and burst into melody, they dance the Sloboviana!

We walked back to the restaurant, which was called the Stopover Café. Nobody was inside except one young waitress sitting at the counter, reading very big book. This book looked very solid and serious. This young waitress looked very big and solid and serious, too, even from the back! Her large and buttery bottom flowed over edge of the stool she sat on like dripping custard.

Looking at the large and buttery bottom of this husky waitress, I naturally thought of Leena Aleenska.

You know, Meero, that I was not sorry to see Leena Aleenska leave our village. Our village fortune-teller predicted at my birth that I was "fated to marry Leena Aleenska, no matter what." This always made me nervous, mostly. And Leena Aleenska never let me forget this prophecy. She would call out to me in village street, "Vospop Vsklzwczdztwczky, you are fated to marry me, no matter what! Don't walk by so fast!"

This does not mean that Leena Aleenska was without feezical attractions! Her thick eyebrows, for example, that met, as eyebrows should, at the center of her nose. Her nose was very fine, too—extremely large and soft and shaped like bathroom plunger. There were also her bazooms, which came in two generous proportions.

And so we walked into the restaurant.

"*Bushweck!*" said my uncle. "I mean, hello good night! We are travelers looking for some fellow illegal Slobovians who might give us shelter."

The waitress poot her book down and swiveled on her stool and looked right at me.

"*Bushweck,* Vospop," she said calmly.

It was Leena Aleenska!

"Leena!" cried my uncle.

"Godfather Shpoont!" cried Leena.

He embraced his godchild and bounced her up and down

21

a few times. Leena then embraced my father and bounced *him* up and down a few times. Even my father rose from the depths of his usual gloom for one moment, seeing a fellow Stoppover. He almost smiled.

Reunion was not so joyous for me, Meero.

"Hello, Leena Aleenska," I mumbled. I like to address Leena as "Leena Aleenska," as you know, because if I call her "Leena," she will tink I am going to marry her, no matter what. I shooked her hand from maybe five feet away. She tugged my arm and with her greater strength pulled me against her.

"Vospop Vsklzwczdztwczky," she veespered in my ear, "you know that you are fated to marry me, no matter what. Destiny has brought us togather again. *Relax.*"

"Is she not beautiful, Vospop?" my uncle said. He inserted his elbow into my ribs and rotated it about ten times. "Look at those eyes! Look at those *biceps!*"

Is true. Leena's biceps are bigger than mine. They strained the sleeves of her blue waitress uniform, just as her plentyfull bazooms threatened to pop the buttons down the front. Everything about Leena is bigger than me. Even her sideburns, mostly.

"But where is everybody?" Uncle Shpoont asked. "Where are the customers? Where are the illegal Slobovians eager to taste homemade horseradish pie?"

"They are all someplace else," Leena said. "They are slouching in doorways, being jobless. No Slobovian can afford to eat at a restaurant. No illegal Slobovian can afford anything. Let's go home to Grandma Aleenska and I will explain."

Leena and Grandma Aleenska lived several streets away,

over an abandoned Slobovian beauty saloon. A sign still hung
in the window.

We Do
Permanents
Temporaries
and
Gone-Before-You-Know-Its

We walked up a dark and narrow and squicky staircase. On
the third floor we entered an *eetski-beetski* apartment, very
neat and spare.

"Leena, is that you?" a familiar voice called from the
kitchen. It was Grandma Aleenska, kneading 28 pounds of
bread dough on the table.

"Grandma Aleenska," Leena said, "look who's here."

Seeing us, Grandma Aleenska stopped and stared, up to her
elbows in the soft dough, like very large marshmallow muff.
She looked like professional wrestler who had just pinned 28
pounds of dough to the mat.

"*Galoshkiss!*" cried Grandma Aleenska.

She embraced us all and bounced us up and down, covering us
with yeasty dough. She covered me with so much yeasty dough, the
shoulders of my blue suit started to rise. Then Grandma Aleenska
made me a cup of onion tea and poured my uncle and my father
a glass of *vottsdott* and fixed us a twelve-course Slobovian meal.
Leena, meanwhile, told us of their voyage to America.

After arriving in their crate of home-dilled peekles, Leena

sold the peekles to a Slobovian blackmarket peekle dealer named Stepin N. Klozdadorski. Stepin N. Klozdadorski knew a good home-dilled peekle when he saw one. On the spot, he proposed marriage to Leena Aleenska. She slapped his face and turned him down because she was fated to marry me, no matter what. With the money from the peekles, Leena opened the Stopover Café.

"The Stopover Café," said Leena, "is soon to be the *former* Stopover Café. No customers, no rent. No rent, no café. The landlord wants to close us down one week from today."

"Leena," Uncle Shpoont said, "why do I see so many illegal Slobovians slouching about in doorways? Why are the streets in the illegal Slobovian section so feelthy? Have my countrypipple lost all their pride?"

"They slouch in doorways," said Leena, "because they can find no work. They can find no work because they are Slobovian. Finding no work, our countrypipple have lost all hope. Having lost hope, they foul their own streets."

"But these are big, strong men! Big, strong women!" said Uncle Shpoont. "What do they do all day?"

"Many turn to crime," she answered. "They become thieves or burglars or smugglers. Some end up in jail. Many are deported. Many end up in jail seemply for standing in a street and being Slobovian! To be Slobovian in America, you see, is to be the lowest of the low. No! *Below* the lowest of the low. You can buy books of Slobovian jokes in bookstores."

"But why?" I asked. "What have we done to deserve such scorniness?"

She shrogged. "*Somebody* has to be the lowest of the low for everybody else to feel good. I guess we were available."

My uncle poured himself some more *vottsdott*.

"And the old Slobovian customs, Leena?" he said.

"Gone," Leena said, "or forgotten."

"The Blessing of the Tires?"

"It does not happen."

"Placing a peeled turnip in one's shoe on New Year's Eve to prevent foot smells, athlete's foot, and toe jam?"

"Forgotten."

"The wearing of the bowling pin?" He proudly displayed his own lapel.

"Unworn."

Grandma Aleenska had begun to wipp into the bread dough. "Is so sad!" she said. "I cry so much, I don't even need to salt the food anymore. The tears are enough."

It was true. The whole kitchen smelled of tears.

Leena patted the old woman's arm. "Donut forget the ancient prophecy," she said. "A red-eyed hero will arrive from Lower Slobovia and create a *New* Slobovia! Maybe the red-eyed hero of Slobovia is here right now!"

She looked straight at me. Her dark, thick eyebrows banged togather like two railroad cars. When she looks at you like that, Meero, you go very small inside yourself.

"Donut look at me!" I said. "My eyes are blue!"

"Hmp," she said, as if I might be lying.

My uncle re-inserted his elbow into my ribs and rotated it a few times. "Is love, Vospop!" he crooned in my ear. "Love!"

The kitchen clock rang midnight. Soddenly I was very exhausted. We had come all the way from Slobovia! Is no small distance.

Leena found blankets and rearranged furniture so that we could sleep on the living room floor. While my father and my uncle arranged their blankets, she pulled me aside.

"So Bilias Opchuck is after you," she said in a low voice.

"You know?" I said. "About the Chiss Poffs?"

She nodded. "Bilias wants his money. Or the Chiss Poffs. Or you three, dead."

All the blood drained from my face into my legs. "I donut know what we're going to do," I said.

"Maybe you can come up with some mad, impossible, insane plan that will save you," she said. Then she pointed to my blankets on the floor. "Sleep now."

"Good night, Leena Aleenska," I said, and she slepped my face.

"What's that for?" I said.

"For just in case," she said.

My uncle and my father and I lay down as we were, too tired to undress. In a moment I had fallen asleep, and Leena Aleenska chased me through my dreams with a giant spatula.

Running even in my sleep from Leena,

Vospop

LADDER FOUR
I Make Unusual Acquaintance

Dear Meero,

Imagine my surprises when I awoke wearing only my underwares. My father Bogdown and my uncle, too, lay snoring in only their undershirts and boxer panties. Clotheslines hung over our heads from every corner of the room. All our dirty socks and the underwares from our suitcases dangled from clothespins. The underwares were washed and starched as stiff as armor. Our shoes, new polished, stood lined up beneath them. Even the laces were polished. Our blue suits and pants and white shirts hung on the shower rod, all cleaned and pressed.

My uncle sat up in his blanket and regarded all this laundry with approval.

"Leena Aleenska," he said, "is a true Slobovian woman! Repulsed by feelth, she can remove dirty clothes from sleeping pipple and never even wake them. She can take the pants off a man without looking at him or soiling her virtue. With Slobovian women, you go to bed feelthy and you wake up clean."

He patted my shoulder.

"You two are going to be very happy togather," he said, "mostly."

"But Uncle," I said, "I am only fifteen! I have all the world to see before I marry!"

"So see it," he said. "*Then* marry Leena Aleenska, no matter what."

"But I donut *want* to marry Leena Aleenska, no matter what. She chased me through my dreams all night with giant spatula!"

"The spatula was clean?" he said.

"Of course! Shining!"

"You want girl to chase you through your dreams with feelthy spatula? This dream is very good sign," he said. He rubbed his hands togather. "Now breakfast. Let's itt."

I poot on a pair of the clean-starched underwares. They gripped my *krotchki* like a nutcracker.

Leena and Grandma Aleenska had laid out a seven-course Slobovian breakfast. Leena had never gone to bed at all, yet she looked very rosy fresh.

"So I hear that you don't want to marry me," she said across the table.

"Leena Aleenska," I said, "you should not overhear conversations you should not overhear. Besides, it is too early in the day for talk about marriage."

"True," Leena admeeted. "We will bicker another time."

"SHE LOVES YOU!" my uncle crooned in my ear for all to hear.

When we had finished breakfast, I said, "Well, Uncle! Now that we are in America, what are we going to do here?"

"We must save somehow the Stopover Café," my uncle

said. "We must also keep from being assassinated by Bilias Opchuck over these Chiss Poffs, for he will keel us in horrible fashion. Today I think I would like to visit with some of my fellow multibillionaires."

"Perhaps," I said, "I should find job. That will help."

"Excellent idea, nephew! I will ask my fellow multibillion-aires if they have anything."

"You will never find a job," Leena said to me. "You are Slobovian."

I felt my angers flare up. Who was Leena Aleenska to tell me I could not find job?

Just in this moment, I saw a huge headline on the front page of the day's newspeeper:

NOAH MCBLOOMINGDALE PROMISES TO CREATE 100,000 JOBS FOR YOUTHS

McBloomingdale Trust Contributes $1 Billion to Create New Programs for Jobless Teens

Underneath the headline was a peekture of this Noah McBloomingdale. He had a face like you see only on money, with very noble nostrils. If this man wanted to be president, you would vote for him for his nostrils. He had nostrils of justice.

"What is this?" I said, grabbing the newspeeper. "Jobs for youths? I am youth! Maybe this Mr. McBloomingdale has job for me! Who is he?"

Leena said, "Noah McBloomingdale is a Texas multibillionaire who gives money to charity."

"Ah," I said, to show how smart I am. "A feelanderopist!"

"Philanthropist," Leena said, correcting me.

"I will go see him," I said, "and ask him for job."

Leena said, "He is multibillionaire! You are Slobovian nobody!"

"It did not stop Christopher Columbus," I said. "It will not stop me."

On a map of the city Leena showed me how the neighborhoods of the city are laid out. The illegal Slobovian section lies betwin the illegal Mexican section and the illegal Polish section and the illegal Turkish section and the illegal Korean and Chinese and Nigerian sections. She showed me how to go by sobway to the legal section of the city, which is very small and hard to find. She also gave me some American moneys and slepped my face, for just in case.

It was nine o'clock in the morning. I was setting off alone into the streets of America, Meero! Too bad my underwares were crunching my *krotchki*!

The running of a harsh and familiar engine caught my ears as I stepped outside. The black Nogo sedan sat idling across the street. The ham-shaped silhouette of Bilias Opchuck filled the backseat window.

I started walking. In a shop window I saw the reflection of the Nogo trailing me. I started walking faster. The Nogo moved faster. I moved faster. Lockily, I heard a crash of gears as the Nogo coughed and died. It was no go for the Nogo.

Then I turned the corner and ran. I ducked down several alleys and jogged across a couple of parks.

When I looked back over my shoulder, the Nogo was now gone. I only needed a sobway to the McBloomingdale Trust Building.

Soon I found a sign for Subway and walked in. Two peemply boys in silly white hats and rubber gloves stood behind a counter among strange phosphorescent foods. They were placing these phosphorescent foods onto bread that looked like a corpse five days dead in a river. Some customers sat at tables chewing these phosphorescent foods.

"Hello good morning!" I said.

One of the peemply pepperoni boys sniggered in his nose.

"Yo, dood!" he called to the other peemply pepperoni boy. "Check out the freak!"

I was surprised that this Subway was a shop for sandwiches and not a train station. Here were sandwiches. Where were all the trains?

I said, "One ticket for D train, plizz." I held out my dollars bill.

The peemply boys both sniggered in their noses.

"Where are *you* from, dood?" the first boy said to me. "Outer space?"

"No," I said. "Slobovia."

"*Slobovia,* huh," said the second peemply boy. "*Kyool!*"

They both sniggered some more.

"So you're a *Slob?*" the second boy said.

"I am not Slob," I said. "I am Slobovian."

"A *Slob*, huh?" said the first boy. "A real *Slob*."

"Gimme five, dood!" the second one shouted.

The two boys five-highed each other.

"*Dood!*" said the one.

"*Kyool!*" said the other.

The first boy, Dood, was so thin he looked like he was hanging on clothes hanger. The other boy, Kyool, had a chin like a pelican and a mouth like a pouch. He had stuffed his huge dreadlocks under an enormous knitted wool cap. He looked like Jiffy Pop.

Clearly, these two boys were complete anuses.

"What have I done," I asked, "that you insalt me? Do you know anything about Slobovia? You have been to Slobovia? Do you speak Slobovian?"

"Look, *Slobbo*," Kyool said to me. "This ain't the subway. And it ain't the *Slob*-way either. This is Subway. Subway *Sandwiches*, O.K.? We make *subs* here. You got it, man?"

"I get it," I said. "I am Slobovian human. You are Subhuman. Goodbye!"

Why did these peemply pepperoni boys, who did not know me or Slobovia, say such things to me? Was it a crime to be Slobovian? What had I done but be born in Slobovia? Were all Americans so stupid and mean?

I was steaming, Meero. I was afire as I walked out. Angry thoughts rotisserated in my brains like bursting wieners as I looked about for the sobway train orifice. It was very hard to see anything, for there were too many advertising signs. Everyplace I looked, somebody wanted me to buy shampoo or computers or saxy lady's underwares or a vacation in Bermuda or better hemorrhoids.

"Can I help you?" a voice said.

A man with a briefcase had seen me and stopped.

"Are you looking for something?" he said.

I pooshed my face into his face.

"I am from Slobovia!" I proclaimed, and beat myself on chest. "Is this a crime, to be from Slobovia?"

Then, realizing my own foolishness, I dashed myself on the forehead with the flat of my hand, in Slobovian fashion.

"Excuse me, plizz, kind sir!" I said. "You are nice enough to offer me help. In return I offer you insalt and act like anus. Pardon my insalt! I am no anus! I am seeking sobway train orifice. I am looking for Noah McBloomingdale."

He smiled and pointed to a stairway at my feet.

"Down there," he said. "Make sure you turn left at the bottom. Get off at McBloomingdale Station."

I shooked his hand. He shooked my hand. We two total strentchers were friends forever for one moment! America is wonderful!

Sobway train is like overground train but without landscape. You stare at black wall, then advertisemints, then more black wall, then more advertisemints. Somebody makes loudspeecher announcements you donut understand. Then you get off. What is porpoise of journey without landscape, Meero?

I emerged in the center of the city. Enormous skyscrappers of glass and granite! Beautiful women wearing telephones on their heads! Men wearing beautiful women on their arms!

A million pipple getting into a million taxicabs and another million pipple getting out! Everybody going someplaces, nobody going noplaces!

Bicycle messengers wearing beckpecks full of beck-peckages zipped by me. How I admired their grace as they threaded through heavy traffic on their delicate bikes! How I loved the sad-eyed young women standing behind cash registers and empty cosmetic counters, gazing longingly through department store windows! How I loved the pipple of all linguitches selling newspeepers and candy at their kiosks, all of them so calm amidst the whirlpool of a million passersby! And the men and women young and old of every color lined up before stores, dressed in their modest best, holding hopeful job applications!

It takes only one American to fill up a sidewalk, for Americans are a wide and well-fed pipple, Meero. And pipple here donut move out of your way on the sidewalk. They walk *at* you as if you must get out of *their* way, as if they owned the world. They have the same stroll as my uncle, who really *does* own the whole world! (In his brains.)

As I walked along, I noticed that Americans are always itting. They itt in restaurants, and in buses; they itt on the street. Ice cream, knishes, fresh-roasted peanuts, Popsicles, pumpkin seeds, soft pretzels, chestnuts, hot sausages, candy bars, gelatos, tacos, Tootsie Pops, sheesh kebabs, falafel, cotton candy, you name it, they itt it—and in public, too! And if they are not itting, they are chewing gum to keep their jaws in practice.

Or else they are drinking! Five-dollar Frappuccinos, bottled water, soda pop, iced tea, **lemonade**, milk shakes, wheatgrass carrot juice, chai, beers in bags, Red Bull, Jamba Juice. Everywhere you go, you hear this sucking sound at the bottom of the empty paper cup. You can stand on any street corner and hear the sound of America sucking.

Meero, if you go into an America pizza place, you donut sit down and itt your pizza slowly. You start to take your next bite while still swallowing the old one! And you walk out the door while still chewing! Unbelievable! The traffic lights here should not say Walk. They should say Swallow.

On one street corner I passed a boy doing what is called *repp.*

"Yo!" he called to me. "My man in blue! With the shiny shoe! And the shiny' do! Are you from Kalamazoo or from Katmandu? What up, Mr. Derring-do? Sock it to 'em, brother! *Hyungh!*"

Meero, this was most beautiful Eenglishes I had heard in my lifetime. I had only two dimes and a neekel extra, but I put them in his cap for giving me such inspiration, and I went my way.

The McBloomingdale Building was 99 stories high and seemed to shoulder all the other buildings aside. (Don't you love it, Meero, that in Eenglish "floors" are called "stories"? For is not every building a heap of human stories?) Inside, the lobby was half as big as all Slobovia and twice as tall. The lobby floor? A vast mirror, Meero. Uniformed guards stood at computers to stop pipple from going in.

"Can I help you?" a guard said to me. But he did not look like he wanted to help me. He looked like he wanted to bitt me up.

"Yes," I said. "I am Vospop Vsklzwczdztwczky."

"Do you have an appointment?"

"Of course not!" I said. "I am nobody. I am looking for summer job."

"Next," said the guard.

"May I plizz speak to Mr. Noah McBloomingdale, plizz?" I said.

The guard laughed. "Hey, Vern!" he called to next guard. "This kid wants to see Mr. McBloomingdale!"

Vern laughed.

"Beat it, kid," Vern said.

I saw then what an anus I am. How could I meet a great, important multibillionaire feelanderopist merely by asking for him? This does not happen in any country in the world. Unimportant pipple are unimportant everyplaces. How Leena would laugh at me when I returned without summer job!

Quite cast down, I turned from the security desk, heading for the street. At the glass doors to the outside, I saw a blond girl in large sunglasses approaching from the other side. Of course, I held open the door for her, of course.

The blond girl reached for the door and fell onto the mirror floor, flat on her faces!

Instantly, we were surrounded. Lights flashed! Sirens sounded! Security guards grabbed my arms! Somebody handcuffed me behind!

The security guard named Vern spoke into a talkie-walkie.

"Get the cops in, George," he said into his talkie-walkie. "We've got a 305 here."

He looked right at me. I was a 305!

"Looks dangerous," Vern said. "Yep. A foreigner."

Another security guard was freesking my body and feeling around my trousers.

"I think he's carrying a weapon, Vern!"

"No!" I protested. "Is only too much starch in my under-wares! Is Leena Aleenska's fault!"

Five police wagons screeched to a halt outside. Twenty police pipple poured out in helmets and machine guns. Working pipple from upstairs were flooding lobby now from the elevators. The whole building was being evacuated because I had opened the door for somebody!

Vern said to me, "You assaulted this young woman and you're going to pay for it big-time."

"I did not assault her," I said. "I held door open for her."

"You *what?*" he said.

"I held door open for her," I said.

"What for?"

"So she could come inside. Instead, she fell flat on her faces!"

News vans pulled up outside. Newspipple poured out with cameras and began snepping peektures. A Hispanic news-caster lady in a red dress and a microphone began to interview eyewitnesses.

"What's up, Vern?" a police captain said.

"This guy says he held **the door** open."

"He *what?*"

Vern said, "He claims he held it open so she could come inside."

"I'll be darned."

"This is America, brother," Vern said to me. "Don't be holding doors open here. It's every door for himself."

The police captain turned his evil eye upon me. "Looks like we got a real live one on our hands. And he sure looks like an illegal Slobovian to me. Say so long to daylight, Slobbo. Adios!"

"Wait!" a voice cried.

The blond girl stepped forward now. She took off her sunglasses and I saw what she was looking like.

She was my age and dressed like a prostitute, mostly. She wore very steep high heels of gold and a *tintski-wintski* gold leather skirt. You could see a black lace brassiere covering her bazooms, which looked like they were somebody else's, mostly. She weighed about 62 pounds. She had three hairs for eyebrows and enough makeup for five other girls, and her gold hair was frizzled like Brillo pad. In short, she was opposite of Leena Aleenska.

"You, like, held the *door* open for me?" the girl said. "I guess you did that because you know who I am, right?"

"No," I said. "I always hold door open for ladies, no matter what."

"So you didn't do it because you're a photographer? Or a gossip columnist? Do you, like, *work* here?"

"No," I said. "I am only polite."

"*Polite?*" she said.

She did not seem to recognize this word. Everybody around her murmured the word among themselves. "*Polite, polite, polite . . .*"

I said, "I came here looking for Mr. Noah McBloomingdale so that I could maybe get summer job. I apology for making you fall flat on faces."

"You mean," she said, "you mean you didn't *know* I'm Tiffany McBloomingdale?"

"No," I said. "Did you know that I am Vospop Vsklzwczdz-twczky?"

"Like," she said, "*wow!* What a name! Where are you from with a name like that?"

I did a despicable thing then, Meero. I said:

"I am from British."

I could not bear to admit that I came from Slobovia, Meero! I had been traumatized by those peemply pepperoni boys and made ashameful!

"Guess I really, like, *fell* for ya, huh, Voss? Ha ha ha." She batted her eyelashes. She had eyelashes as thick as Bulgarian pitchforks from mascara. "If you read the rags, you'll know it won't be the first time I fell for a guy."

"I donut read Rags," I said. "Only Shiksepeer and Dostoyevsky."

"You are so *kee-yoot!*" she said, as one says of leetle dog before he urinates on you.

Tiffany McBloomingdale did not have American vowels. She had Californian vowels. I had heard many blond girls in swimsuits with such vowels on my uncle's 24-Hour American Commercial Channel. She said "nuh" instead of "no," "yuss" instead of "yes," and "good" rhymed with "did." Whenever she said "whatever," which was often, the word was five *r*'s long. "What-*ev*-errrrr." It was very deefeecold to understand her, mostly. Her exsent was too strong!

The police captain blew his whistle. "O.K., folks, clear it up! Back to work!"

"What happened here?" a passerby said to the police captain.

"Guy opened a door for somebody," the captain said.

"Unbelievable!" the passerby said. "Was he a foreigner?"

"Yeah."

The crowds began to disperse and I was left alone with Tiffany McBloomingdale and the hundred photographers taking her peekture. She did not seem to notice them.

"So you wanted to meet Dad, huh?" said Tiffany McBloomingdale. "Come on up. I'll introduce you."

And she took my arm and headed me for the elevators!

Unbelievable, Meero. Only one day out of my freight container and I am meeting the great and powerful Noah McBloomingdale! A man of inhuman charity! A person who has dedicated his whole life to piss on earth!

This demands some exaggeration points!!!

Your over-excitable friend,

Vospop

LADDER FIVE
I Meet a Multibillionaire and Almost Get Shot

Dear Meero,

Tiffany McBloomingdale breezed past the security guards, who gave me hairyful eyeballs while I passed.

"He's with me," Tiffany told them.

We rode up to the 99th floor in an elevator bigger than my entire house in Stoppova. This was Tiffany McBloomingdale's personal elevator. It had a television with stock market reports to tell me how much money I was not making. While we rode, Tiffany McBloomingdale looked me up and down and in betwin, with a smiling on her faces.

"So tell me," I said. "Why do so many American girls dress like prostitutes?"

The elevator doors opened and everybody on floor 99 heard me ask this question. A hundred heads turned and looked at me. Tiffany McBloomingdale laughed.

"You're so kee-*yoot!!*" she said, in her California exsent. "Hi, everybody! This is my new friend Voss. C'mon, Voss!"

She led me into a huge office with a view that made me deezy. The city's buildings, streets, and river were laid out beyond the peekture windows like Monopoly pieces.

Two men stood facing away from us, watching an enormous television on the wall, like movie screen. One man wore a gray suit. One man wore a blue suit. This man in the gray suit also wore silver cowboy boots that looked like they were made of real silver. When he turned to us, I recognized his nostrils. They were the nostrils of Noah McBloomingdale.

"Hiya, Daddy!" Tiffany said.

"Howdy, hun!" Noah McBloomingdale boomed in a drawl. "We was just watchin' ya on television!"

It was very strentch. Tiffany talked like somebody sucking on helium in California. Her father talked like Texas cowboys. You see, Meero, in America you have many United States in one family!

The enormous television was showing news report from the lobby of McBloomingdale Building. The Hispanic lady in the red dress and the microphone was speaking to camera.

The Hispanic lady said, "Tiffany McBloomingdale, the media's teen-queen darling, got a shock today when a *total stranger* opened a door for her, here in her father's 800-million-dollar McBloomingdale Building . . ."

All the channels were showing Special News Flashes from the lobby of the McBloomingdale Building. None of these news flashes showed me. They showed nothing but Tiffany McBloomingdale. Once you saw my nose, only. It poked into the side of the peekture like tip of garden hose.

"You weren't hurt, were ya, Tiff?" Mr. McBloomingdale said. "I was purty dang worried."

"*Da-a-d,*" she said, and rolled her eyes and made stupid faces. "*Duhhh!*"

They laughed. In America, is polite to tell your parent he is stupid.

Tiffany pooshed me forward. "This is the guy who did it, Dad. This is Voss. He's British."

Noah McBloomingdale held out a hand to me. His hand was as big as all Arizona. He shook my Slobovian hand and almost broke my bones.

He said, "Openin' a door like that for a stranger. Why, it's wonderful, Voss. *Wonderful!* It's traditional. It's old-fashioned. It's generous and moral and all the other things we love in this country. Y'er a gentleman, that's what you are. A true gentleman. Must be that old-school British upbringing. I bet you pull chairs out for women at tables, don't you."

"Yes, sir," I said.

"I thought so. I bet you walk on the curb side of the sidewalk when y'er walkin' with a lady."

"Of course, Mr. McBloomingdale!" I said.

"You hear that, Tiffany?" he said. "You hear how he calls me 'sir' and '*Mister* McBloomingdale'? You see how he's wearin' a suit and a tie and a clean white shirt? And shoelaces? Do you know how *rare* that is these days?"

"Don't you just, like, love him, Dad?" Tiffany said.

"Tiffany," he said, "I do. He's a very enterprising and sensitive and cultivated young man. I like that, son. I like that a lot!"

He called me *son!* This exuberant billionaire man who is opposite of my gloomy father. I am only one day in America and a reetch feelanderopist is calling me *son*. O America! Land of offertunity! I open a door, and the doors open for me!

"Now I want you two to meet my new friend," said Noah McBloomingdale.

The man in the blue suit turned around.

Mr. McBloomingdale said, "This here is Mr. Shpoont."

It was my Uncle Shpoont!

"Galoshkiss!" I cried.

"Hello, Vospop," said my uncle. Then he bowed and kissed Tiffany McBloomingdale's hand.

"How do you like my building?" he said.

Noah McBloomingdale laughed and patted Uncle Shpoont on the back and winked at us.

"You ain't gonna get my building out from under me *that* easy, Mr. Shpoont!"

He laughed and my uncle laughed and they patted itch other's back.

"You see, Tiffany," Noah McBloomingdale said. "Mr. Shpoont's got a lotta holdings around the world."

"Yes," said my uncle. "I own it."

This only made good Mr. McBloomingdale laugh more loudily. He and my uncle patted itch other's backs like peekpockets.

"He's been givin' me all kinds of business advice," said Mr. McBloomingdale.

My heart stank. My crazy uncle had been giving beeznest advice to Noah McBloomingdale?

"The man's a financial wizard!" Mr. McBloomingdale boomed. "I said the words *U.S. Steel* and what did he say?"

"Buy," said my uncle.

"I said *Xerox,* and Mr. Shpoont said what?"

"Sell."

"Well, I called my stockbroker and I give him these orders. I made a cool *billion* just in the last ten minutes on this advice! What should I do now, Mr. Shpoont?"

"Buy," said my uncle.

Mr. McBloomingdale picked up the telephone and talked to it.

"Murray?" he said to the telephone. "Buy! Buy up! Buy everything!"

He poot the telephone down.

"Sell," my uncle said.

Mr. McBloomingdale picked up the telephone.

"Murray?" he said. "Sell!"

He listened for a minute and a grin brightened his face. He poot the telephone down.

"I just made FOURTEEN BILLION DOLLARS, Tiff!" he said. "*Whoo-EEE! Yippeeeeeeee! Yippie ai oh kai ay! Whoop whoop whoop! Hot dawg! Hot dangit, hot dawgit, hot diggety DAWG!*"

Any minute, I thought, he will take out a lassoo and rope some cattle.

"Maybe you'd like to contribute a piece of all them holdings o' yours, Mr. Shpoont," said Mr. McBloomingdale. "So I can give some of it away to charity."

"My pleasure!" said my uncle, and they laughed and patted each other some more. "In the meantime," my uncle said, "here is contribution for you. And something for your daughter."

My heart stank again as my uncle took out his coin purse. He took out a button and handed it to Tiffany. Then he took out another and handed it to Mr. McBloomingdale. It was all over now. Mr. McBloomingdale would know that my uncle was no multibillionaire, but crazy person! These were buttons from some old Slobovian long johns!

"God, Daddy, look!" Tiffany squealed. "Isn't it *cool?* It's this, like, *antique button!*"

"Beautiful, beautiful," said Noah McBloomingdale, turning the thing over in his hand. "Just beautiful! Thank you, Mr. Shpoont! I'm honored."

"Donut spend it all in one place," said my uncle.

"Daddy," Tiffany said, "Voss came here looking for, like, a summer job."

"He did, did he? Well, I think I can find something for a well-mannered young man. So here's an idea, Voss: Why don't you squire my unruly daughter around town and keep her outa trouble? That's a challenge for an enterprising young fella. 'Cuz I gotta warn ya, Voss—she's *frisky!*"

He poot his arm around his daughter and kissed her chick.

"Dad-*dee,*" she said. "Don't be such a jockstrap."

In America is polite to call your parent a jockstrap. In Slobovia, not so much, mostly.

Mr. McBloomingdale said, "Now, Voss, we gotta talk

about compensation. So how 'bout if I start you off at a salary of . . . Well, what would you say to a hunderd thousand dollars a year?"

"ONE HUNDRED THOUSAND DOLLARS A YEAR?!" I said.

"That's right," he said. "Whaddya say, Voss?"

"I will take it, mostly!" I said. "I say thank you!"

"Excellent! Welcome aboard, son." (He called me *son* again!) "Now if you'll excuse me, I gotta give away a few billion dollars to charity. Then I'm goin' to lunch with Mr. Shpoont here so him and me can talk *money*. See ya round the ranch, Voss!"

My legs were made from robber, Meero! I was to squire Tiffany McBloomingdale around for $100,000 per year. And I did not even know what squiring was!

If my summer job lasted three months, I would make one-quarter of one hundred thousand dollars per year. This equals $25,000 for summer job. Not so bad! (Or maybe $100,000 is normal for American summer job?) My only worry was that Uncle Shpoont would go to lunch with Mr. McBloomingdale and Mr. McBloomingdale would realize that my uncle was, as we say in Slobovian, *lunitunz*. Then he might take my $100,000 summer job away.

Only one day in America and I am worried about losing $100,000 summer job! Already I am having American dream, and I am not even American!

With such moneys I could maybe save the Stopover Café. I could also maybe start to pay off the blackmarket imitation Chiss Poffs.

This reminded me of Bilias Opchuck. As Tiffany and I walked out of the McBloomingdale Building, I looked up and down the street for a black Nogo. No Nogo was nowhere not to be seen.

"Here's my limo," Tiffany said. "Care to start *squiring?*"

A silver limousine sat at the curb with a chauffeur in uniform who held the door open for us. His name was Carlo and he had stobble like you see in advertisemints for underarm deodorants.

Meero, this car had everything except toilet. You needed binoculars to see Carlo in the front seat, he was so far away. The leather seats were as black as licorice and even softer.

The minute we drove away, Tiffany jumped on my body and locked her leeps to mine. Soddenly I had her tongue in my lungs!

I stroggled. Her legs held me clamped. I tried to cry out. Her leeps held me tight. Meanwhile, her hands tested my principles. Lockily, I was wearing virtuous Slobovian clothing, starched by Leena!

I threw her off.

"What you are doing?!" I cried. "I donut know you!"

She stared at me, amazed. "You mean you don't want to?" she said.

"Want to what?" I said.

"Like, *wow*," she said. "I *do* love you!"

She tried to jump on my body again. I was too kveek. I scampered like squirrel into the corner and wiped her leepstick from my face. She opened her *tintski-wintski* purse and took out fifty kinds of makeup.

"I'm kinda hurt," she pouted. "But I'm also, like, *so IMPRESSED!*"

While she replaced her face, she told me about her spring vacation. She had been to Miami Bitch, London, France, Italy, China, Australia, New Zealand, Fiji, Brazil, Tokyo, Patagonia, Kenya, India, Alaska, and South Pole.

"Where is Patagonia?" I said.

"I dunno," she shrogged. "I think it's in, like, Central America someplace. Anyway, it's like real bleak and rocky."

She had been everyplaces but did not know where anyplace was. She waved Patagonia away. "What-*ev*-errrrr," she said.

The backseat of this limousine was littered with magazines. Tiffany's face was on every cover, with a different boy. "Tiffany Breaks Up With Justin." "Tiff Has Tiff with Orlando." "Billionaire Princess Breaks Elijah's Heart." "Are Tiff and Tommy in Trouble?" "*I Want Carlo's Baby,* Says Tiffany McBloomingdale."

"You want Carlo's baby?" I said. I pointed to the chauffeur. "This Carlo's baby?"

She laughed. "Oh, come on, Voss. I was *misquoted.* Duhh!"

Here is this *duhh* again. In America, insalting people is polite!

I picked up her gold perfume bottle. On the front, it said, *GOD. By Tiffany.* Her leepstick and purse said the same thing. *GOD. By Tiffany.*

"What is this?" I said. "*GOD, by Tiffany.*"

"My line of cosmetics and accessories," she said.

"Called *God?*" I said.

"Pretty brilliant, huh?"

"You cannot call face powder *GOD!*" I said. "You cannot call purse *GOD!!!*"

"Why?" she said.

"Because only God is God! God is not handbag!"

She leaned in very close and curled up like a cat.

"You're so, like, *deep,*" she said.

I was shocked, Meero. Yet I could not forget what her leeps felt like, pressed to my leeps. Or her tongue like a cat's, licking in my lungs. This had never happened to me before, to have a girl jump on my body like that. Eenteresting sensations, Meero!

Tiffany wanted to go shopping.

First she bought some fleep-flops such as cleaning ladies wear in Slobovia and buy for five *slotkeys.* She paid 700 dollars. She then decided my polished black shoes with shoelaces were too "uncool." So Carlo drove us to a *ritzki-fitzki* shop where Tiffany bought me a pair of one-thousand-dollar Gootchi loafers. These were so soft and delicious I did not want to wear them. I wanted to itt them.

She then bought me a peegskin wallet and a thousand-dollar wristwatch and a celephone. This celephone had a

Global Positioning System so that I would always know where Tiffany was or *vice-a-verski*. She had one like it from her father, in platinum. He loved her so much he wanted to know where she was every minute of the day.

Tiffany and I went for ride in her private helicopter. We flew over the city and Tiffany again tried to jump on my body, this time at 5,000 feets. Again I pooshed her off me. Is very tiring, pooshing pipple from off your body!

Then Tiffany took me for sailing on her own private yott. This yott is so long, it looks more like bridge. I was exhausted from having so many funs.

It was evening when we returned to illegal Slobovian section of city. Tiffany pressed her face to the limo's windows.

"I've never seen, like, so many men in hats," she said. "Are they all British, too?"

"Yes," I lied. Is good thing her geography is so bad!

Carlo stopped in front of Leena's building. Pipple filled the doorways and windows up and down the street, staring at the limousine. Tiffany was oiling her leeps with more God-by-Tiffany leepstick.

"See you tomorrow, Voss," she said. "Nice and early."

She leaned forward very slowly to kiss me and, Meero, I was very, very, very tempted. But that was when a shot rang out and a bullet shattered one of the windows. The bullet flew through the limousine and out the window next to me. The bullet came so close I could feel the breeze the bullet made on my teeth.

I looked out the shattered window and saw a black Nogo

sedan roar away up the street, with a hamlike head in the backseat.

The past was catching up, Meero. The Chiss Poffs were taking their revenge.

Getting leetle more worried,

Vospop

LADDER SIX
Leena Shoots Me, Too

Dear Meero,

You remember I was in silver limo being shot at. Even in America this does not happen *every* day. I know this because Tiffany McBloomingdale jumped up and banged her golden hair on roof of limo. Lockily, her hair is so frizzy. Also, her limo is padded and bang-proof.

"What was *THAT?!?!*" she said.

"Nothing," I said.

"Nothing" was easier to say than "a bullet fired by Bilias Opchuck because of some Chiss Poffs." I wondered if I had lost my job.

"Was that, like, a *bullet?*" she said.

"Yes," I admitted.

"God," said Tiffany. "I *LOVE* IT! You sure are full of surprises. I can't wait to see what happens, like, *tomorrow!*"

She drove away and I sat on the front stoop to digest all the happenings of my day. I set my old black uncool shoes beside me. They were like my own Slobovian ghost, with shoelaces.

Leena walked up wearing the blue uniform of the Stopover Café. The streetlights were just coming on.

"Hello, Leena Aleenska," I said.

She burst into tears.

"You've met somebody else!" she wailed, and began to wipp. She knew about Tiffany just by looking at me. She has Slobovian female radar mechanism.

"Leena," I protested.

She began to tear out her hair.

"I!" she sobbed. "I, who was fated to be Leena Vsklzwczdztwczka! Now I will never be that!"

"Leena," I said, "calm down! I have met nobody! I have gotten summer job for $100,000 squiring Tiffany McBloomingdale around! You see this good news? The Stopover Café is saved!"

Then she saw the Gootchi shoes on my feet.

"What is this?" she cried. "*Gootchi*? And *loafers*? A man is not a man who does not tie his own shoes! And a man is not a man who dumps his future wife-to-be, no matter what!"

"Please, Leena," I begged. "Be calm!"

She stopped wipping and took a dipp, dipp breath. As she did this, a button popped from the bazoom of her blue uniform and flew at me like bullet. It struck me in the ribs. I took out the ancient family pocket watch from my pocket. The face of the pocket watch was shattered. The hands were stopped. They waved like drowning pipple calling for help.

"There," she said. "Now your pocket watch will always say 9:09—the moment at which you broke Leena Aleenska's heart."

Where the button had flown off her uniform, the blouse had opened to show her heavy-duty white robber brassiere underneath. As I say, Leena Aleenska was the opposite of Tiffany.

Leena saw me staring and covered herself, crossing her arms over her bazooms. "Is she beautiful," she said, "this Tiffany McBloomingdale?"

"Is hard to tell," I said. "She dresses like prostitute, mostly."

"I knew she was beautiful," Leena said. "Did she jump on your body?"

"Yes," I said. You cannot lie to Leena. She will keel you.

"Who can blame her?" Leena said. "Except me?"

She stomped back and forth up and down the street, making great noise in her Slobovian shoes. Indeed, Leena's feet stamped out the rhythm of our ancient Slobovian love ballad, "Angry Woman, Stupid Man." This is the song with the chorus, *You're in the soup, you're in the soup, she's waving her iron spoon, you're in the soup and drowning.* Listening to the sound of her shoes, I felt like what Americans call a heel.

Just then another limo pulled up. This limo was platinum and wore a pair of giant, pointy cattle horns on the front bumper, like raging bull. My Uncle Shpoont stepped out, with Mr. McBloomingdale behind him. They were returning from ten-hour lunch, their faces flosh from expensive foodstuffs.

"Well, pardner," said Mr. McBloomingdale, slapping my uncle on the beck. "That was one heck of a lunch. One! Heck! Of! A! Lunch! Whaddya say?"

"Sell," said my uncle.

"I can't sell." Mr. McBloomingdale laughed. "The market's closed!"

"Buy," said my uncle.

"I'll buy first thing in the morning," Mr. McBloomingdale said. Just then he spotted me on the stoop. "Howdy, Voss! How's tricks?"

"Who is Tricks?" I said.

"HAR HAR HAR," said Mr. McBloomingdale.

He laughed and pounded my uncle on the beck some more. My uncle pounded him beck. Leena paid them no attention, still stomping out Slobovian love ballads in her shoes. This caught Mr. McBloomingdale's ear.

"That's one musical young lady there," Mr. McBloomingdale said. "Somebody oughta promote her. She could have a real career! G'night, Mr. Shpoont!"

"Bye," said my uncle.

"I tell ya, I *can't* buy. Oh, you mean g'*bye*-bye! My mistake! A little too much veeno at yer restaurant! Bye, now!"

"Bye!"

"Bye!"

"Bye!"

They kept yelling "bye" at each other. Or maybe "buy." I could not tell. Mr. McBloomingdale rode away in his platinum bull car.

"What time is it, nephew?" my uncle asked.

"I donut know," I said. "Leena Aleenska shot my watch with her bazoom."

"Ah, young love!" he sighed and frisked up the ends of his handlebar eyebrows.

"Uncle," I said. I wanted to tell him about the bullet that almost drilled my teeth.

"You should have seen my restaurant," my uncle interrupted. "Incomparable cuisine!" He kissed the tips of his fingers.

"Uncle," I said.

"Also," he broke in, "my French tailor shop, where Noah ordered me some suits."

My Uncle Shpoont and I were certainly running in some reetch circles.

"Also," he went on, "there was my gas station, where we filled my tank."

Truths to tell, I was getting rather tired of my uncle's properties.

"*Uncle,*" I interrupted his interruption.

Just then a window shot up above us and Grandma Aleenska poot her head out.

"Vospop!" she said. "Come kveekly! Your father is very seek!"

Racing up the stairs,

Vospop

LADDER SEVEN
Pilgrim's Paradise

Dear Meero,

I ran into the apartment behind Grandma Aleenska, with Leena and Uncle Shpoont close behind.

"Poppup!" I called. "Are you there?"

My father Bogdown was dragging himself, wheezing and hacking and coughing, from the bathroom. He looked sweaty and baggage-eyed and flushed as if with high fever. Perspiration plastered his thick hair to his skull.

"Poppup!" I said. "What is wrong?"

He dropped into the armchair like sack of dying potatoes. When he breathed, you could hear wet oysters flapping in his lungs.

"We must take him to one of my hospitals," my uncle said.

"We can't take him to a hospital," Leena said. "We are illegal. We will be deported. Besides, we have no health insurance. In America, only reetch people can afford to be sick."

"What do other illegal people do when they get seek?" I said.

"They die," said Leena.

"Perhaps we should stop at one of my drugstores," my uncle said.

"Please, Uncle," I cried. "For heaven's sake!"

"Just a suggestion," he shrogged.

Once again my eye fell with a bang upon the day's newspeeper. Below the article about Noah McBloomingdale was an enormous advertisemint.

Are You POOR?
Are You ILL?
Do You Need a *HELPING HAND?*

――――――――――― COME TO ―――――――――――

PILGRIM'S PARADISE!

• Free Health Care •
• No Questions Asked •
• No Strings •
• No Costs •
• And No Fees! •

"There is our solution!" I cried. "We must take him to this Pilgrim's Paradise!"

While Leena gathered some moneys, I wrapped my father in blankets to keep him warm. Two minutes later we were all in the street.

"I must find one of my cabs," my uncle said.

Just then, a taxicab screeched to a halt before us.

"*Ohmygodyes!*" said taxicab driver. It was Mr. Awakan Singh, taxi number CO1935! This is what Americans call great coincidence. This is what, in other countries, pipple call unbelievable. But in America, Meero, *anything* is believable. They have no time here for unbelievable!

We all piled into the back, Grandma Aleenska and Uncle Shpoont, too. I was pressed up so close against Leena, in Slobovia we would be legally married and could go on honeymoon.

"To the Pilgrim's Paradise!" I cried to Mr. Singh. I thrust the newspeeper with the address into his hand. "As fast as you can, please, Mr. Singh. My father is deathly seek!"

He tore away. You have heard of the blind leading the blind, Meero? This was the Sikh driving the seek.

Some streets later, Mr. Singh peered into his rearview mirror.

"We are being followed by a black Nogo," he called back to us.

"Lose him, plizz, Mr. Singh," I said. "This Nogo is up to no good."

Mr. Singh did lose him, by going up to 80, 90, 100 miles per hour. We threaded through the steel girders of roaring elevated trains. We just missed mothers with baby carriages and old ladies with shopping carts. We overturned fruit stands. All the things you see in American movies, Meero? We did them! I was in movie!

Finally, we pulled up before a beautiful modern building, nine stories high, as white as a tomb, with golden doors. Some perfect flowers grew in perfect flowerbeds out front. A sign said, "Pilgrim's Paradise. A Helping Hand for the Needy."

Mr. Singh would not take our moneys.

"Go!" he said. "Hurry! Your father is seek! You have no time for losing!"

"How do you like my building?" my uncle asked him.

"Uncle, please!" I said. "Not now!"

The cab drove off and we bundled my father Bogdown toward the entrance.

The golden doors sleed open automatically, like a mouth about to swallow us. Another, darker pair of doors stood closed before us now. The golden doors sleed shut behind us without a sound. We stood as if trapped in the entranceway, which was very quiet and white and fluorescent. The darker doors remained closed before us.

"*Welcome,*" a voice said from the ceiling. A quiet, calm, friendly female voice. "*Who are you?*"

"Good evening hello!" I shouted to the ceiling. "We are pilgrims in need! My father Bogdown is very seek! Plizz, help us!"

I had the feeling that this room was looking at us, maybe even photographing us.

Then the darker doors sleed open, revealing a large, empty white lobby. A starchy white nurse stepped toward us, carrying her thin, pale hands like a nun. Her spongy white shoes made no sound at all on the polished floor, as if she were floating. She was as white and silent as cottage cheese. Her name tag said, Jane Ashcroft, Registered Nurse.

"Can I help you?" she said.

I removed my gray fedora hat. This was a chance for me to use my Eenglishes.

"Yes, plizz," I said. "My name is Vospop Vsklzwczdztwczky. I see by the name on your bazoom that you are a nurse."

Leena poked me and veespered, "Vospop! You don't say *bazoom*!"

"I correct myself," I said. "I see by the name tag on your bazooms in plural that you are a nurse. This is my father Bogdown Vsklzwczdztwczky. He is very, very seek."

My father stood collapsing betwin Leena and Uncle Shpoont. Grandma Aleenska wipped into her fingers as if this were the end of the world. I scented her sweet Slobovian tears.

The nurse touched my father's forehead and checked his pulse.

"We are illegal Slobov—" I began.

The nurse held up one of those nun-like hands and stopped me.

"We ask no questions here about your private circumstances," she said. "We only want to help you."

She looked at my father carefully. Her eyes were pale gray, like metal.

"Is your father's health normally like this? Is he subject to illnesses?"

"Never!" I said. "He is undefeated Tree-Throwing Champion of Lower Slobovia. He was never seek a day in his life until America!"

This seemed to impress Nurse Ashcroft.

"He seems a perfect candidate for Pilgrim's Paradise," she smiled.

I heard the *squick, squick, squick* of a squicky wheel. A hunchbacked man in a white jacket appeared, pooshing a gleaming hospital cart with a spotless mattress.

"John," Nurse Ashcroft said to him, "this gentleman is quite ill. Please help Mr. Vsklzwczdztwczky onto the gurney."

She called my father a gentleman. And she could pronounce our name, Meero! What a wonderful woman! What a wonderful place! America was heaven. Everything was fibulous!

"We have no moneys," I began. Again Nurse Ashcroft stopped me with a raised hand.

"There are no fees here," she said. "No bills. No costs whatsoever. We are a charity institution."

By now my father Bogdown was lying on the gurney and ready for his journey.

"Must he be strapped down like this?" I said. For John the orderly had strapped my father down so hard that my father could not move.

"That's for his own safety," said Nurse Ashcroft. "We don't want any accidents, do we?"

"Should we not fill out some peepers?" I said.

"To protect your privacy," she said, "we have no paperwork. Thank you, John. Please take Mr. Vsklzwczdztwczky upstairs."

I tasted tears in my throat like acid. Soddenly I could not bear to see my father go.

As if she had read my brains, Nurse Ashcroft said, "Dr. Washington will look at your father immediately, Vospop. Don't you worry about a thing."

Dr. Washington! What a fine traditional American name! Yet why did this foolish fear tug at me, Meero? Why did I feel so uneasy?

Once again reading my brains, Nurse Ashcroft said, "Would you like to see some literature about Pilgrim's Paradise?"

A brochure appeared in her fingers like sleight of hand. You should have seen this pamphlet, Meero! Deluxe hospital rooms! Olympic-sized swimming pools! A gleaming, shining kitchen! A gymnasium where patients on treadmills looked healthier than me! Room service waiters delivering heaping trays of food to patients in glistening hospital beds! All of this in fool Technicolor!

"May I go upstairs with him?" I said. "My father and I have never been apart a single night of my life."

"I'm terribly sorry," she said. "Not at this hour. You can come back and visit him tomorrow, anytime between nine and six."

Still this uneasinessness tugged at me, Meero. My father lay staring up at the ceiling and wheezing.

"Donut worry, Poppup," I said. "All will be well."

I expected some gloomy Slobovian proverb. Instead, he said to me in Slobovian:

"Take me away, Vospop. Donut leave me here."

"Is O.K., Poppup!" I said in Eenglish. "Everything is A-OK! This place is perfect! Everything here is perfect! The rooms are perfect! The swimming pool is perfect!"

Then he did quote an old saying.

"Perfect," he said, *"is a lie. They're going to kill me."*

John pushed the gurney through some swinging doors.

My Uncle Shpoont asked Nurse Ashcroft, "How do you like my hospital?"

She smiled her ghostly smile. "I like it very much."

She pointed us all toward the dark doors to the outside. As she did so, the doors opened as if on signal.

"Thank you for bringing us Mr. Vsklzwczdztwczky," she said. "We'll take very good care of him."

Still I hesitated before walking out those dark doors.

"You have done a good thing, Vospop," Leena assured me.

And I thought, *Yes, Vospop, relax. You have done a good thing.* Why, then, did I feel so uneasy? My father's words echoed in my brains: *Take me away. Donut leave me here.*

They're going to kill me.

We walked out the dark doors. I turned and watched them shut without a sound, erasing Nurse Ashcroft from sight. Then the outer, golden doors opened and we walked out into the night.

Somehow, Meero, I knew I had made the most horrible mistake of my life.

Too choked up to go any further,

Vospop

LADDER EIGHT
A Restless Night

Dear Meero,

That night I tossed around on the floor until my blanket wrapped me like straitjacket. In the pale darkness I could see my father's blanket, folded and hung over the arm of the couch like a flag after a soldier's funeral. His empty pillow had the hard, finished look of a tombstone.

About three o'clock in the morning I could toss no longer. I needed air. I needed space. Quietly I poot on pants and shirt, slipped out of the apartment, and climbed the hallway stairs to the roof of the building. A gray haze had erased the sky.

I stood at the edge of the roof and looked eastward—toward Slobovia, toward you, Meero, toward our old house, somewhere beyond the curve of the earth. In Slobovia it was morning already! You were leading George Clooney into the field and leaving a trail of fragrant cow pies behind you. I felt homeseek, Meero. Homeseek, and lonely, and afraid.

"*Bushweck,*" a voice growled behind me. I heard the *cleek* of a peestol. "Poot up your hands."

I raised my hands and turned around. I expected the ham-shaped head of Bilias Opchuck. But this head was a smaller ham—the discount size.

"You are not Bilias Opchuck," I said.

"No," the hamlet said. "I am Stepin N. Klozdadorski. The illegitimate *son* of Bilias Opchuck. I tink you owe my father some Chiss Poffs."

"We can pay him back!" I cried. "I have summer job for one hundred thousand dollars!"

Stepin N. Klozdadorski sneekered.

"Yes," he said, "taking care of this pinheaded princess. An insalt to Leena Aleenska!"

"So it wasn't Bilias Opchuck," I said. "It was *you* who almost shot me in the back of Tiffany McBloomingdale's limousine."

He exploded with rage.

"You are unworthy to marry Leena Aleenska!" he said. "*You* don't love her! *I* love her!"

"Good!" I said. "That's wonderful! I love that you love her!"

"If you like it so much," he said grimly, "you can help me."

"Anything!" I said.

"Leena Aleenska believes that she is fated to marry you, no matter what. If you convince her to marry me someday instead, I will convince my illegitimate father to forgive your debt. He will forget about the Chiss Poffs. He will forget about the money. I will give you four days to convince her. If not, at midnight three days from now, my father will keel you in horrible fashion. He will not keel your uncle, who is notts. Nor your father, who is gloomy and blameless. But *you* he will keel. He will core you like apple, Vospop Vsklzwczdztwczky!"

"Three days?" I cried, picturing this apple. "Three centuries are not enough to convince Leena Aleenska to marry you!"

"Three days from now, at midnight," he repeated. "Or *apple.*"

He turned and vanished down the stairs into the building. I heard the cough of a Nogo driving away up the street.

You may well imagine that I did not slipp this night, Meero. In my brains I only saw myself cored like apple. Is no pretty peekture, mostly!

Just after dawn I heard Leena get up and start making a seven-course Slobovian breakfast. I went in and leaned in the doorway, watching her work.

"Funny thing," I said. "Just by coincidence I ran into Stepin N. Klozdadorski last night!"

Leena said nothing. She banged some pots around the stove.

"What a nice boy he is!" I said. "So friendly! So sweet! So kind! So thoughtful! So generous! So . . ."

"So?" she said.

"He loves you," I said.

"I am fated to marry *you*," she said, "no matter what. Which means I marry you even if I like you or not. As it happens, I love you."

"But *I* don't love *you*," I said.

"So?" she said.

"Stepin is handsome," I lied. "I am hideous! I am unsightly! I am plain! I am so-so!"

"So?" she repeated. "I choose you. Even if you are hideous and unsightly and plain."

This was leetle bit insalting.

All through breakfast, I continued my campaign. I praised Stepin N. Klozdadorski every chance I had. I praised his looks, his voice, his character; I praised his success as blackmarketeer.

Grandma Aleenska stared at me rather funny. "Vospop," she said slowly, "are you in love with Stepin N. Klozdadorski?"

"No," said Leena, "Vospop wants me to marry Stepin N. Klozdadorski. But I will *not! Never! Ever!*"

I would be cored like an apple.

The telephone rang. Everybody jumped, for this telephone never rang.

"Hello?" Leena said to the telephone. She held it out to my uncle. "Is Mr. McBloomingdale, for you."

My uncle took the telephone and listened to it for a minute.

"Sell," he said, and hung up.

The doorbell rang and I jumped across the room. You see how jumpy I was. But it was only Carlo the chauffeur, to take me away for squiring.

Leena followed me outside, curious to see this Tiffany. Truths to tell, I was not so much in mood for squiring today. I had my father all the time at the back of my brains and Stepin N. Klozdadorski at the front of my brains, with much confusion in the meedle brains.

Tiffany stood waiting at the curb. Today she did not wear a silver limousine, for the silver limousine had bullets through the windows. Today she wore a gold limousine.

Leena and Tiffany faced off on the sidewalk like angry chickens.

"You must be Wiener," Tiffany said.

"*Leena,*" Leena corrected her. "You must be Tacky."

"*Tiffany,*" Tiffany corrected her. "What a, like, *interesting* dress you have on there. What's that made out of? Tungsten steel?"

"I would comment on your dress," Leena countered, "but I cannot see it. I will have to find my microscope first."

"Is that, like, your hair," Tiffany said, "or a helmet? Voss, shall we, like, go?"

"*Beckwash*, Leena," I said.

"Hmp," said Leena Aleenska.

"What's *beckwash*?" Tiffany said to me as we got into limo.

"Is British," I said, "for goodbye."

The minute we drove away, Tiffany jumped on my body. I freed myself and straightened my hat and my blue suit and my necktie. I then sank into the black licorice seats as one sinks into gloomy thoughts.

"What's the matter, Voss?" Tiffany said. "Are you bored? Are you depressed?"

I shrogged. I did not want to tell her about my father Bogdown, for my father was Slobovian and I was supposed to be British. I also did not want to tell her I was going to die for marrying Leena Aleenska. It was all too complicated.

Tiffany took out her platinum celephone and called a friend. You see, Meero, in America it is O.K. if your friends are boring or deep-pressed. All you do is take out celephone and talk to somebody else instead.

First Tiffany wanted to have brunch. *Brunch* is American for "waste of time." Brunch was two hours. Then she had pedicure. This was one hours. Then she wanted to have lunch. We drove two hours to a *fantski-pantski* lunch place. Lunch was three hours, though she ate only one walnut off her Waldorf salad and sent back the rest. Reetch pipple seem to live in restaurants, mostly. In the meantimes, I only got more jumpier and gloomier than I was before.

Then we went to art show opening.

Tiffany had a "dear, dear" friend who was artist. A very, very famous artist, too! I had never heard of her. This artist was named Sasha Blah. Today was the big splashy opening of Sasha Blah's exhibition at the National Institute for the Totally New and Cool, known as NITNAC.

We drove into *artski-fartski* part of city that used to be warehouses and workers' housing. Now it has Art and is too expensive for workers.

Outside NITNAC, a huge banner said "Blah: The New New Works." Inside, everybody was dressed in black, like for funeral.

Sasha Blah, too, was dressed in black. Her black was blacker than anybody else's. I noticed that she had a brown, sausage-shaped tattoo on her shoulder. While she chattered with Tiffany, I pozzled over this tattoo. The knobbly brown sausage looked familiar, but I could not recognize it entirely. I looked around at her paintings instead.

Her paintings were all of turds! These turds were maybe three feet long and very juicy-looking. Here the turd was pink, here it was yellow, here it was blue, here it was purple, here it was green. There was also extra-large brown turd. The brown turd had been sold to a Japanese billionaire for sixty million dollars for his living room.

The pipple in black went from painting to painting, from turd to turd, sipping white wine and comparing the turds. Most of the pipple liked the pink turd the most. A lady in trifocals who was art critic reviewed the turds with notebook and pencil.

"These are all turds!" I said.

"Yes," said Sasha Blah. "It took me years, but I finally found my subject."

Then I realized that the brown sausage shape on Sasha Blah's shoulder was a turd, too. A turd tattoo. A turdtoo.

"C'mon, Voss," Tiffany said. "Let's look around."

I did not want to look at turds. All my jumpy gloom began to bubble inside me. What was I doing looking at colored turds when my father was seek in hospital?

"YOU CANNOT MAKE PEEKTURES OF *TURDS!*" I said. Everyone turned around and stared at me. "*YOU CANNOT WEAR A TURD ON YOUR SHOULDER!!!*"

"Sure you can," Tiffany said. "It's *art.*"

"Art is not turds!" I said. "Except sometimes by accident!"

"What-*ev*-errrrrr," Tiffany shrogged.

When we got back into the limousine, Tiffany said, "You know, you really, like, embarassed me in there."

"These peectures were turds," I said. "Is dizzgusting!"

"I don't, like, *care*, Voss! I thought they were beautiful!"

"O.K.," I said. "Beautiful turds. I can look in toilet and see this every day."

"I can't *stand* you!" she snepped. "I hate you! I hate you!"

Now I snepped, too, Meero.

"O.K.," I said. "I resign. Here! Take your Gootchies!"

I tore off the Gootchi shoes and threw them across the limousine. I then threw my peegskin wallet and my thousand-dollars wristwatch and my celephone with Global Positioning System. I surprised myself how angry I was. I would have thrown myself from my own skin, but I was stuck inside it.

"By the way," I said, "I am not British. I am Slobovian!"

"NO!" she screamed. Her face crumpled up in dizzgust. "You mean . . . You mean I've been hanging out with a SLOBOVIAN?"

"Yes," I said. "An illegal Slobovian. I sheeped myself to America in freight container with Chiss Poffs."

"EEEEEEEEUWWWWWW!" she moaned.

I gave Carlo the address of the Pilgrim's Paradise. I had decided that I would take my father home now, no matter what. I did not care about police or deportation. I only wanted him back with me where we belonged.

Tiffany took out her celephone and called me names to some friends of hers. She was still calling me names when we pulled up at the Pilgrim's Paradise. I got out of the limousine in my stockings feet.

"Goodbye," I said. "Thank your father, plizz, for this job."

The limousine roared away. Only two days in America, Meero, and I lost $100,000 job!

The Pilgrim's Paradise looked different somehow in daylight. It looked more larger and less friendly. Again the golden doors sleed open like a mouth. I stood in entranceway before the darker doors.

"Welcome," the ceiling said. "Who are you?"

"I am Vospop Vsklzwczdztwczky," I said. "I have come for my father Bogdown."

The dark doors ahead of me remained closed.

"I was here last night," I said. "You remember? My father was very, very seek."

The dark doors remained closed.

"Plizz!" I called out. "Let me in!"

I began to bang on the dark doors, calling, "Let me in! I want my father!"

The dark doors sleed open and I found myself face-to-faces with Nurse Ashcroft. "Hello," she said calmly as if she had never seen me before. "Can I help you?"

"Nurse Jane Ashcroft!" I said. "I am Vospop Vsklzwczdztwczky. I brought my father Bogdown here last night. I want to take him home, plizz."

"What was the name?" she said.

"Vsklzwczdztwczky," I said.

"I'm sorry," she said. "We have no one here by that name."

"Nobody here?" I said. "But you saw him! You were here! I was here! You remember me, Nurse Ashcroft! You sent my father up to Dr. Washington!"

"Nurse who?" she said.

I looked then at the name tag on her bazooms.

It said, R. A. Damantis, Registered Nurse.

"Damantis?" I said. "But your name is Ashcroft . . ."

"You mentioned," she said, "a Dr. Washington? We have no Dr. Washington on our staff. Dr. Sarkoffagis is our staff physician and surgeon. Obviously, you have the wrong place."

"No! I was here!" I said. "Just last night!"

At this moment, John the hunchbacked orderly walked through in his white intern's jacket.

"*John!*" I called to him. "You see? There is John! He will remember me! He was pooshing the gurney with the squicky wheel."

The nurse motioned John over. "Igor," she said to him while pointing at me. "Who is this?"

"I don't know," the man said, studying my face. "I've never seen him before in my life."

"This is nightmare!" I said.

"Thank you, Igor," the nurse said. "That will be all."

Igor alias John disappeared through the swinging doors.

"But my father Bogdown . . ." I stammered. "My father . . ."

The nurse held up that soundproofing hand and stopped me.

"I must ask you to leave, young man. Or shall I call the police?"

"Yes!" I said. "Call the police—"

I stopped myself. Of course she could not call the police. I would be arrested. They would tink I was crazy anyway! How could I convince them that my father had even been at Pilgrim's Paradise? There were no peepers, Meero. No records. There was nothing. *Neetchi.*

"Good luck finding your father." The nurse smiled.

She turned away on her soundless shoes. Then the dark doors closed, shutting me out.

Beffled and afraid,

Vospop

LADDER NINE
The Turtle and the Straws

Dear Meero,

Out in the street, the perfect flowers were blooming all around me in their perfect Pilgrim's Progress flower beds. Meanwhile, my father was missing! How could these two things happen at the same time?

I sat down on the curb before the Pilgrim's Paradise and poot my head in my hands. I wanted to cry, Meero. I wanted to scream. I must have looked very gloomy, because a strentcher stopped and crouched down beside me. He was kindly faced and looked like turtle.

"You O.K., kid?" the turtle asked me. "Is something wrong?"

"Yes," I said. "Today is the worst day of my life."

The turtle held up a finger, as if I had given wrong answer.

"No, no, no," he corrected me. "Today is not the worst day of your life. *You HOPE that today is the worst day of your life.*"

The turtle patted my shoulder and went his way.

This is comfort? This was no comfort. This was deezying thought, Meero. Very feel-low-sophical! And I was soon to find out that this turtle had been right.

It was supper by the time I had walked home. My socks

were in rags and my feets were torn and bloody. Grandma Aleenska heard me come in. She walked out of the kitchen carrying five pounds of red, raw, glistening steak, like a beef muff. I marched around and around the living room in a frenzy, kicking things.

"Vospop!" she said. "What's the matter? Why are your feet so torn and bloody?"

Uncle Shpoont heard all this and came in, too.

"Vospop!" he said. "Why are you marching around and around the living room in this frenzy? Why are you kicking things?"

Grandma Aleenska began wipping and calling out my name and dabbing her eyes with the meat.

"Vospop! Vospop!" she wailed. "Speak! Say something!"

How could I tell them? How could I say that my father Bogdown had disappeared? How could I tell them that he had disappeared from a place *where I myself had poot him?* And how would I ever find my father? How would I find out what had happened to him?

The door opened. A young lady of my own age entered, wearing an *eentski-weentski* gold dress. She had a great shelf of bazoom and enormous hips and buttox and was shaped like fire hydrant. Her thick dark hair was frizzled like Brillo pad, and instead of eyebrows she had pencil drawings. Her leeps were as red and steeky as candy apples. She teetered on high-heeled gold sandals made of air, mostly.

"Leena Aleenska!" I cried. "What has happened? Where are your eyebrows?"

"Do you like it?" she said. "Do you like me?"

"No!" I said. "You look like fire hydrant on stilts!"

"But I thought . . ." she stammered. "I thought that since you liked Tiffany McBloomingdale . . ."

She bursted into tears and melted her makeup.

". . . I thought you would like me like this!"

"Leena, I have beef, if you want to cry into it," said Grandma Aleenska. She gave Leena the meat muff, and Leena cried into that.

"I only wanted to make you love me," Leena said, dabbing her eyes with beef. Now the beef got all the makeup, so that Leena's face with a leepstick kiss was printed on the steak.

"But Vospop," said my Uncle Shpoont. "You were marching around and around the living room in a frenzy. You were kicking things."

"A frenzy?" Leena said, soddenly sober. "Kicking things? Why? What happened?"

I told them, Meero. I told them everything that had happened at the Pilgrim's Paradise. When I finished, they stared at me aghastly.

"Bogdown?" said my Uncle Shpoont in a wondering tone. "Disappeared? From *my* own hospital?!"

This was my last straw. I had already been losing straws all day. Beware of person with no straws, Meero. He keel you!

"*Your* hospital, Uncle?" I exploded. "It is not *your* hospital! It is not your anything! *Nothing* is your anything! You own nothing, do you hear me? Not buildings, not bridges, not Coca-Cola Corporation! You are penniless immigrunt with only some old buttons to your name! You have nothing! *I* have nothing! We all have nothing! And my father, God help him, he has more nothing than any of us, for he himself is missing!"

My uncle stared at me, Meero. He stared dipp, dipp into my eyes. His own eyes grew into two large, black zeros in his face.

"Nothing . . ." he echoed in a dazed and hollow voice. "Nothing . . ."

He looked about himself, as if seeing this place for the first time.

"Yes," he nodded slowly. "You are right, Vospop. I have nothing."

He slumped into the armchair and stared before himself. This was the same chair where my father Bogdown had slumped in gloom. Now my uncle, my joyous uncle, had slumped into it and taken my father's place.

I knelt before him.

"Forgive me, Uncle," I said. "Forgive me. It was cruel from me. I had lost all my straws. That's all."

He only stared at the wall, saying, "Nothing . . . Nothing . . ." over and over again.

The telephone rang. Leena answered and held the telephone to my uncle.

"Mr. McBloomingdale," she said. "For you."

My uncle shooked his head.

"I am not here," he said. "I am not home. I am nothing."

The Turtle and the Straws

   Leena gave the telephone her regrets and hung up. In my head I heard the voice of the turtle, promising worser days to come.

   Pulling into my shell for now,

Vospop

LADDER TEN
I Have Crazy Plan

Dear Meero,

So there we were. My Uncle Shpoont slumped in his chair, saying, "Nothing, nothing." Leena staring at the telephone as if it might have answers. Me, still kneeling by my uncle, exhausted from problems. Only Grandma Aleenska remained calm and wise, which is the job of grandmothers everyplaces.

"Come into kitchen, Leena," she said. "First we must itt. Then we must tink."

Nobody spoke at the table that evening. My father's empty chair seemed to reproach me. Where was my father gone? Was he alive? Would I never hear his gloomy proverbs again?

We had been fooled, Meero. Fooled by the beautiful surface of this Pilgrim's Paradise. By perfect promises and perfect peektures in fool-color brochures. My father had even tried to warn us. *Perfect is a lie,* he had said.

"But *why* were we fooled?" I wondered outloudski. "What is the secret of all this? What is this Pilgrim's Paradise behind its white facade?"

"We can never find these things out," Leena said. "We would have to get inside."

"Then I will go inside," I said.

"But how?" Leena said. "They have seen you, Vospop. They will recognize you."

This was when I had my inspiration, Meero.

"I have a plan," I said.

"Is it an impossible plan?" Leena asked. "A mad plan, an insane plan?"

"Yes."

"Good," she said.

"I will disguise myself as all-American boy! I will go in disguise. I will get a job in this Pilgrim's Paradise and snick around. If my father is there, I will find him."

"But if they catch you, Vospop—" said Grandma Aleenska.

"This is the risk I must take," I said. "Is our only chance. I will do it tomorrow, mostly."

What did I have to lose, Meero? In three nights Bilias Opchuck would core me like apple anyway.

The next morning, Leena and I went out to buy me a disguise.

In a discount store we found me some all-American-boy clothes: a hooded gray sweatshirt and a baggy pair of jeans five sizes too big. They kept falling down behind so that you could see my crevasse. We also found a baseball cap five sizes too big and a pair of real imitation Nike snickers with no shoelaces. I also bought a chipp set of earphones. You cannot be an American boy without wearing earphones. We did not have enough money for iPod or disc player, only for headphones.

Lastly we bought a beckpeck. In America you must wear a big beckpeck so that you can bump into other pipple on the bus and sobways. I had nothing to poot in this beckpeck. We filled it with bricks from a construction site.

When I poot on these clothes, I looked like real clown, Meero. I looked like rumpled bag with earphones. An all-American boy.

"You have to bop your head," Leena said, "as if to music from the earphones."

I bopped.

"Now you have to wreegle your body and snep your fingers," she said.

I bopped. I wreegled. I snepped.

Leena handed me some Wreegley's Juicy Fruit gums.

"Now chew," she said.

I bopped. I wreegled. I snepped. I chewed. Is very hard to bop and wreegle and chew while keeping your five-size-too-large pants up. Especially when you are wearing a beckpeck filled with bricks.

I was exhausted by now already. Is very tiring being an American boy, Meero!

As we walked toward the sobway, I practiced bopping and wreegling and snepping. At the sobway orifice, Leena looked me down and up one last time.

"You look very stupid," she said.

"Good," I said. "If they are doing something illegal at this Pilgrim's Paradise, they will welcome stupid workers. Stupid workers donut notice anything. They donut talk about nothing either."

"What you are doing is very brave, Vospop," Leena said. "We will talk about this often, after we are married."

I said, "Are you sure you don't want to marry Stepin N. Klozdadorski instead?"

"Good lock," Leena said. *"Husband."*

"Eesh," I said.

I descended into sobway orifice. Twenty minutes later I stood before the Pilgrim's Paradise. As I approached between the perfect flower beds, the golden doors sleed open. Pulling down the brim of my baseball cap, I went through the golden doors and stood in the entranceway before the darker doors. I could feel the ceiling watching me. I bopped. I wreegled. I snepped. I chewed.

"Welcome," said the ceiling. *"Who are you?"*

"Yo, dood!" I called out. "I am, like, looking for summer job, whatever! You got any jobs here, dood?"

There was a long silences. Then the voice said:

"Go around the back and ask for Mr. Stoodgly."

"Kyool!" I said. "Whatever, dood! Like, check it out, mostly!"

I bopped and wreegled back into the street and around the corner. Behind the Pilgrim's Paradise, I found an alley full of broken glass and dog turds. (Not Art, this time. Real turds, with smell.) In the meedle of this alley was a shabby, peeling door. A sign said:

PILGRIM'S PARADISE
EMPLOYEE ENTRANCE
Trespassers Will Be Prosecuted
To The Full Extent of the Law
KEEP OUT

Very different from the perfect front of the building! There were no flowers here, only dog turds. No golden doors, only warnings.

A burly, unshaven man in a rumpled security guard uniform leaned against the wall, smogging a limp and soggy cigarette. I wondered why the Pilgrim's Paradise needed a security guard at its back door. What was this guard keeping out? Or in?

I bopped up to him.

"Yo, dood," I said, "I'm, like, lookin' for Mr. Stoodgly."

He growled something around the soggy cigarette and jerked his dirty thumbnail to the shabby, peeling door. I walked through it, into the Pilgrim's Paradise kitchen.

You remember the gleaming, shining kitchen I told you about from pamphlet, Meero? This was no gleaming, shining kitchen. It was a hellhole, dark and feelthy. The stoves and sinks dripped with old, moldy, crusted foods. Ants and cockroaches swarmed over everything. A brown beetle as big as my thumb swam the American crawl in a cauldron of old, cold, greasy soup on the stove. The fluorescent lights in the ceiling fleekered constantly.

"Hello, there!" a cheeriful voice called out. "Can I help you?"

A short, chubby, bald man had come out of an office next to the kitchen.

"Yo, dood!" I said. "I'm, like, looking for, like, a summer job? They said to, like, ask, for Mr. Stoodgly, whatever, mostly."

"I'm Pat Stoodgly." He grinned. "C'mon into my office!"

A sign on the office door said P. STOODGLY, HEAD OF NUTRI-TIONAL SERVICES. Inside this office was only a desk, two chairs, and a metal food chart hanging on the office wall. Magnetic metal foods stuck to the chart.

"Excuse me a second, will you?" Mr. Stoodgly said. Humming a cheeriful tune, he bustled over to the board and moved the magnetic metal vegetables around like pieces on a chess-board. Mr. Pat Stoodgly was one of those pipple who is so cheeriful he seems brainiless.

"Broccoli . . ." he muttered. He moved a magnetic broccoli. ". . . and *pork chops* . . ."

He moved a magnetic pork chop. He rubbed his chin with one hand while absentmindedly scratching his testiculars with the other. He seemed to be completely seempleton.

"Yams?" he said. "Yes! *Yams!*"

He switched the magnetic yams and the broccoli.

"Do you know anything about nutrition?" Mr. Stoodgly asked me, pointing to the board.

"Nothing, sir," I said.

"Just remember this," he said. *"Fiber is our friend."*

"Kyool! I will rememorize that!"

"Fiber," said Mr. Stoodgly, "helps you move your bowels. Do you move your bowels regularly?"

"I move them all the time, sir." (What is bowels, Meero?)

"Good!" he said. "So you're looking for a summer job. Take a seat!"

We sat at his desk. He almost disappeared.

"What's your name, son?" he asked me.

I had to tink fast for good American name to hide my true identity.

"Tom Sawyer," I said.

Mr. Stoodgly looked quite surprised at this name.

"Tom Sawyer," he said, "like the book?"

"What book?" I said. "You mean *The Adventures of Tom Sawyer,* by Mr. Mark Twain? I donut know this book."

"Say, what's that accent you've got?" he asked. "Where you from, Tom?"

I thought fastly again.

"Pittsburgh," I said. "Wisconsin."

"Do you have any experience as a room service waiter?"

"Much," I said. "*Much* much."

"You know," he said, "it's only minimum wage here."

"I love meenymum wages!" I cried. "I am meenymum person myself!"

"When can you start?"

"Right now today this minute."

"Excellent! Let's get started, then."

He rose to go.

"Should I not fill out some peepers?" I said.

"No, Tom," he said. "We don't bother with paperwork here. Orders from up on top."

He solemnly pointed upwards with one hand and scratched his testicular with the other. (Is very hard to do at same time, Meero!) Mr. Pat Stoodgly was a perfect person to be working at the Pilgrim's Paradise. He was so seempull he would notice nothing. He would not see the mold on the stoves or the brown beetle swimming in the soup. Plus, he had his magnetic vegetables and his testiculars to play with.

"You'll be working with Zack and Shawn," he said. "They're in the pantry. Come on and meet 'em. Let's get to work! *Chop chop!*"

Mr. Stoodgly took me into a very large freezer room filled to the ceiling with white boxes like shoe boxes. This was the pantry. The white boxes were crudely stamped with the word LUNCH. Two boys were piling them onto wheelycarts. Like me, they wore gray hoodie sweatshirts and jeans five sizes too large that showed their hairy crevasse. They too snepped and wreegled and bopped their heads to headphones.

"Zack and Shawn," said Mr. Stoodgly. "This is Tom Sawyer."

The boys did not even look up.

"Dood," said Zack.

"Kyool," said Shawn.

Could you believe it, Meero? They were the two peemply pepperoni boys I met from Subway Sandwiches!

"*Galoshkiss!*" I said in surprise. Then I covered that with, "Wow, man! Tubular, mostly!"

"Show Tom the ropes, will you, boys?" said Mr. Stoodgly. "He'll be helping out on room service."

"Kyool," said Shawn.

"Dood," said Zack.

"Welcome aboard, Tom!" said Mr. Stoodgly. "Now get to work, boys! *Chop chop!*"

He went back to fight his magnetic vegetables.

"Guess the Stoodge likes ya, huh," said Dood. His real name was Zack, but in my brains he would always be Dood.

"Whatever!" I said. "So what do I, like, do, dood?"

Dood said, "You, like, put these boxes on this cart and then we, like, wheel 'em up to the freaks."

"Freaks?" I said. "What are these freaks?"

"The freakin' *patients,* dood! The idiots upstairs."

I began to heap lunch boxes onto another wheelycart. I looked inside one of the boxes. There was one tiny, dried sandwich. One tiny, wilted, dead, green vegetable. There was one ancient brick of dried cake. So this was the garbitch they served to patients?

While I loaded my wheelycart, Dood and Kyool horsed around, five-highing each other and acting like anuses. I learned from their conversation that they had been fired from Subway Sandwiches because they could not poot pepperoni on sandwiches properly.

"Hurry up, man," Kyool said to me. "The faster we deliver this crap, the sooner we're done. You take the second and third floor. We'll take the rest."

"Kyool, mostly!" I said. "But listen, have you ever seen this man?"

I took out a peekture of my father taken at the Festival of

Saint Slobovius. He was, of course, wearing the traditional cast-iron skillet, which is the symbol of Saint Slobovius.

Dood sniggered. "This dood is wearing a frying pan!"

I ignored his snigger. "Have you ever seen him?" I said. "Is he a patient here?"

"What're you, nuts?" Dood said. "Like we're gonna pay attention to who's up there? You think we, like, *care* or somethin'?"

They were too stupid even to be interested in why I was asking. I poot peekture away.

Behind the kitchen was a corridor with the service elevator, a big steel cage maybe one hundred years old. We got in with our wheelycarts and Kyool rettled shut the folding gate. The elevator shrieked and groaned and slowly rose. Outside the cage, the bare brick walls of the elevator shaft went down as we went up. The walls dripped with something bleck as tar.

The elevator screamed a leetle as it reached floor two.

"What do I do?" I said.

"Whaddya think, man?" Kyool said. "Knock on a door and take in the box and get the fork outa there. Go up and down the corridor and do the same thing. Like, whatever!"

"Go on, dood!" Dood said.

I pooshed my loaded wheelycart out of elevator. The elevator headed up to the next floor. I was alone.

I stood in a dark corridor—so dark I could not even make out the color of the walls. Doors ran up and down both sides of the corridor. At the end of the corridor, a bend led to more corridor and more doors. The fluorescent lights fleekered here, too, buzzing and humming. Something slithered along the baseboard and ran over my feet. It was a rat as big as cocker spaniel.

The whole corridor was moaning, Meero. Moans and groans and faint cries for help came from all the rooms up and down the corridor. And this was where I had left my father!

I knocked at room 201.

"Lunch!" I cried, rather foolishly.

I heard nothing from inside. I turned the knob and went in.

An ancient dirty hospital bed. Bare walls, the color of snot. A grimed-over window that looked out onto nothing. The only light came from a dark bulb dangling from a bare wire from the ceiling. In the bed a man lay, moaning.

He was strapped to the bed so that only his hands were free to feed himself. When he saw me, he began babbling in some linguitch that was not Eenglish. He kept trying to tell me something.

"Is O.K.," I kept saying. "Is O.K. I am friend."

Still he babbled in his linguitch, tugging my arm, desperate to tell me something. Shocked and ashamed, I left him his lunch and went to room 202.

Every room was the same. A man or a woman lay strapped to a bed. They were Mexican and Korean and Chinese and Ethiopian and Brazilian and Russian and from every nation of the world. Every one of them tried to talk to me. Every one of them begged me for help in every linguitch of the world. I tried to say that everything was all right and that help was coming. But everything was not all right. No help was coming.

What was the meaning of all this, Meero? Why was Pilgrim's Paradise taking pipple as patients and mistreating them?

Around the bend of the corridor, I passed the doors of another, more modern elevator that did not look like a service elevator. I wondered where that led to. When I walked into the next room beyond the elevator, the woman strapped to the bed whimpered with fear.

"*Galoshkiss!*" she breathed as I walked in.

She was Slobovian, Meero!

Spitchless,

Vospop

LADDER ELEVEN
Dr. Sarkoffagis

Dear Meero,

I stood shocked in doorway, unable to believe any of my ears. A fellow countryperson, Meero! A Slobovian woman, speaking my linguitch!

"You say *galoshkiss*?" I cried to the woman in the bed. "I say *bushweck*!"

She made big-big scream.

"You are Slobovian?" she cried out.

"Yes," I said, "my name is Vospop Vsklzwczdztwczky."

"Of the Vsklzwczdztwczkys from Stoppova?"

"Yes!" I cried. "How did you know?"

"I am from Leftova!" she said. "Two villages over! Do you know Lilka and Lilka?"

"Of course!" I cried. "Their cousin Meero Mrkz is my best friend! I am writing him every day."

Her stricken face crumpled and she began to wipp.

"Who are you?" I asked. "How did you get here?"

"I am Erica," she said. "Erica Mannska. Two months ago, I and my husband, Tomas Mannsky, smoggled ourselves over to America.

"Oh, Vospop," she said, "we were so happy to be here! So eager to be free and equals! But we kveekly realized that we

94

were not free and equals in America. We were Slobovians. Tomas was expert metalworker back in Slobovia. He was artist, Vospop! Tomas could write your name in steel as easily as you do it with a pen! Here, he could find no work. No one would hire him because he is illegal Slobovian. He was nothing.

"Soon," she went on, "my husband was reduced to stealing hubcaps. Then, one week ago, I fell and cut my leg. You see, Vospop?"

She showed me a long, ugly, open wound that ran down her calf from ankle to knee. Yellow pus oozed from it. She needed help for this leg and she needed it soon.

"Tomas saw an advertisemint for this Pilgrim's Paradise. *No costs, no fees, no strings* the advertisemint said. So he brought me here and we met this nurse.

"She promised me good medical care and a beautiful room. I said goodbye to my husband. Then this orderly, he brought me to this room and locked me to this bed and left me. Otherwise I have seen no one but these two boys who bring me food."

She began to wipp again.

"Why has my husband abandoned me, Vospop?" she wailed. "Why doesn't he come and see what this place is and take me away?"

"I think I know why," I said. "Because he doesn't know you're still here."

I told her about my father. I was sure that what had happened to me had happened to her husband, Tomas. I then related to her how I had disguised myself as an all-American anus so that I could find my father and rescue him.

"Do you know him?" I asked her, showing her his peekture. "Have you seen him here? Bogdown Vsklzwczdztwczky?"

"I have seen nobody," she said, "except those two boys and that witch, who comes in here once a day, checks my pulse, nods her head, and leaves."

"And this doctor?" I said. "Dr. Washington, or Dr. Sarkoffagis? What do you know of him?"

"I have never seen him. But *why*, Vospop? Why do they do all this?"

"I donut know," I said. "I hope to find this out."

She lowered her voice and stared at me with fear in her wide-open eyes.

"Sometimes, Vospop," she veespered, "sometimes I hear screams. I hear screaming in the corridor."

A cold, kveek sheever ran down my spine and out my feets.

"I swear to you, Erica Mannska," I said, "that I will help you. Now I must go before they suspect something. Courage! *Beckwash*, Erica!"

"*Beckwash*, Vospop," she said. "God bless you!"

I rushed through the rest of the second floor, delivering the white boxes. Every room I entered, I hoped I would meet my father. But he was nowhere.

I returned down the service elevator to the pantry and loaded up my wheelycart. Mr. Stoodgly came in.

"Tom," he said, checking his watch, "you're going to have to work faster than this. You're way behind."

"Excuse, plizz!" I said. "I got, like, lost in the upstairs. I am okeydokey now!"

"Now finish off these lunches! *Chop chop!*"

"Yes, sir!" I said. "I am chopping!"

I raced through floor three, knocking on doors and calling out, *"Lunch!"* This was deefeecold, because I was wearing five-sizes-too large trousers and snickers without shoelaces and a beckpeck filled with bricks. In every room, some poor person lay trembling in a wretched bed. In every room, somebody grabbed my hand and tried to talk to me, babbled in his or her linguitch, begging for help. And I had been wasting my time riding in helicopters and wearing Gootchi shoes! With such misery and cruelty in the world!

I was walking out of a patient's room when I heard a scream that curled my blood.

The scream of a man in terror.

The blood froze in me, Meero! I wanted to run, but my feets were stuck to the floor and my heart was glued to my ribs. Then I heard voices around the bend of the corridor— voices and the *squick squick squick* of a squicky wheel on a hospital cart.

Nurse Damantis came into view, floating on her silent shoes. The blazing white of her cap and uniform and pale stockings made her glow like a ghost in this dark corridor. At her back was Igor, pooshing the gurney.

A man lay strapped down on the gurney, screaming out his lungs.

Usually a nurse comforts a frightened patient. Usually a nurse says, "Don't worry, everything is going to be all right." This man screamed, and Nurse Damantis said nothing. She merely strode before him, heartless on her soundless shoes. The man might not even have been there.

They came closer and closer but did not see me yet in the dimness.

There was another person in this group. In the fleekering lights I only saw him on and off, on and off, washed in light, then vanished in darkness. He wore a tight black suit and strode with his head down, intent as a spider. His long legs in his narrow black trousers were like spiders' legs, too. Just like a spider, he sensed me before he saw me. He looked up and stared right at me from behind the small, square lenses of his spectacles.

I knew instantly that this was Dr. Sarkoffagis.

I moved aside to let them by, bopping my head and snepping my fingers so that I looked like anonymous anus.

"Doctor . . ." the nurse said, to warn him I was watching.

"Kyool!" I murmured. "Like, whatever."

"It's all right, Nurse," the doctor said. He had a voice without moisture, as hard and dry as stone. "Merely one of our mindless drones."

The man on the gurney then saw me. He tried to speak Eenglish.

"Help me!" he shouted. "Help me! They are going to kill me!"

"Shut up!" Igor growled. The man stopped screaming and only whimpered instead.

"Please . . ." the man begged me. "*Please . . .!*"

"Kyool," I muttered. "Whatever, dood . . ."

Igor pooshed the gurney into the service elevator. The elevator shrieked and groaned all the way down to the basement. I wondered what was in that basement.

I heard the folding gate open and then close down there.

Then there was only silence.

Rettled,

Vospop

LADDER TWELVE
A Narrow Escape

Dear Meero,

In the kitchen, Mr. Stoodgly waited for me with his watch in hand.

"Much better, Tom!" he said, very cheeriful again. "Excellent time! Record-breaking! Keep up the good work! Now help Zack and Shawn unload that truck outside, then help yourself to some lunch. And feel free to use the Employee Dining Room!"

A large black truck was parked in the alley outside the kitchen. It had brought the boxes for the next day's breakfast, lunch, and dinner. Dood and Kyool and I transferred the boxes from the back of the truck into the pantry. When we finished, we could have "lunch," as Mr. Stoodgly said, in the "Employee Dining Room."

Lunch meant one of the white boxes with dried sandwich, dead vegetable, and ancient cake. The Employee Dining Room meant a room that smelled like old underwares, with a long, rickety table and some broken folding chairs. When you dream about dying, you dream about a room like that, only nicer.

After Dood and Kyool ate their ancient cake and sucked their straws dry, they took out some veedeo games. Boys here spend many hours staring into these leetle plastic veedeo boxes, kill-

ing cartoon soldiers or driving cartoon racing cars and pooshing buttons that go *bipp bipp bipp*. These veedeo boxes hypnotize
you like voodoo. Maybe they should be called voodeo games.

Making their *bipp bipp bipp*, Dood and Kyool paid me no
attentions or each other. In America is O.K. to sit at table with
somebody and not talk to him. I sat with my lunch box and
no appetite. In my brains I could still see this screaming man
on the gurney.

"What do we do now?" I said.

"Nothin' till supper," Kyool said. "Then we do the same
crap all over again. Take the supper boxes up, pick up the
lunch boxes, feed the freaks, and forget about it."

"They are not freaks!" I shouted.

I reached across the table and grabbed Kyool by the neck
of his sweatshirt.

"These pipple are not freaks! They are human beings!"

"Whoa!" he said, trying to back up. "Cool it, man! Cool it!"

I was in such a rage I really tink I could have keeled him
at that moment, Meero. For he was not only insalting all the
patients upstairs. He was insalting that man on the gurney
and he was insalting my lost father, too.

"What's with you, dood?" Dood said.

"Nothing," I said. *"Dood."*

I let him go and we sat in sober silences, as pipple do right
after violences. I sat listening to the mindiless *bipp bipp bipp* of
their voodeo games. My white lunch box sitting on the table
before me looked to me like a small white cardboard coffin.

I could not sit there doing nothing. So I left the Employee

Dining Room and stood quietly listening in the corridor that ran behind the kitchen. I could hear Mr. Stoodgly in his office, humming his cheerful tune. My coast was clear.

I called the service elevator. My heart beated fast again and my guts boiled and churned and I tasted that nauseating fear smell in my nostrils. I have always been a coward, Meero. But I could be one no longer. I was an illegal immigrunt, and nobody could be brave for me.

I got out on floor four. Dim, dirty, fleekering, just like floors two and three. Here, too, you heard quiet calls for help in every linguitch on earth from the doors up and down the corridor. Here, too, rats and vermin scuttled along the walls and floor.

Kveekly and quietly I went from doors to doors, looking in. My father was in none of the rooms. I rode up to the fifth floor. Again I went from rooms to rooms, opening doors, looking in, closing doors. Still no father.

I walked around the bend in the corridor.

"What are you doing here?"

Nurse Damantis stood before me with arms folded. I had not heard her on her silent shoes. Her level, colorless gaze bored through my eyes into the back of my brains.

"Yo!" I said. "Hey, Nurse Damantis! Da praying mantis! Da queen of Atlantis! What up, girl? *Hyungh!*"

While I repped, her eyes narrowed.

"I asked you what you're doing up here instead of down-stairs where you belong."

I had to think fast. "I like lost my iPod, see?" I said. I held up my earphones to show the nothing on the end. "What a bummer! You seen my iPod, Nurse Damantis? Gotta be around here somewheres."

I looked around the floor like my missing iPod might be there. Locky thing for me I could not afford iPod. My poverty saved me now!

"What's your name?" she said.

"Thomas Sawyer," I said.

"What's in the backpack?"

Deefeecold question, Meero! If she looked in my backpack, this would give away my disguise!

"Well?" she barked. "What's in the backpack?"

"Bricks," I said. "For building strength. Very good for back muscles! Also, very good for moving bowels! You should try this. You will move yours all the time!"

She studied me one more minute. "Go back downstairs. And mind your own business."

"Sure thing, Nurse Damantis. Whatever! And hey, if you see my iPod, let me know, O.K.?"

I left her standing there. I could feel her brains tinking about me.

Dood and Kyool were still going *bipp bipp bipp* in the Employee Dining Room. I threw myself into a chair and sat tinking for one minute. I had to find my father, dead or alive. What if he was not upstairs at all? What if he was hidden in secret hiding places in this building?

"What is in basement?" I asked.

"Huh?" said Dood.

"What is in basement of this building?" I said.

"I dunno," Kyool shrogged. "Nobody's allowed in the basement."

Instantly, I was interested. "Why not?" I asked.

"I dunno."

"How do you get to basement?" I said.

"We call it '*the* basement,' not 'basement.' The service elevator'll take you there. Or you could take the stairs. But like I say, nobody's allowed."

"What stairs are these, plizz?"

They rolled their eyes to tell each other I am stupid.

"The stairs through the doors at the end of the *hall*," Kyool said. "Only you can't take 'em 'cuz nobody's, like, *allowed* down there. How many times do I gotta tell ya? Jeez!"

I headed out again.

"Thank you," I said, "for the warning."

At the end of the corridor I found a black door with a pooshbar and a sign. ABSOLUTELY NO ENTRY. I could still hear Mr. Stoodgly humming his cheerful tunes in his office, busy with his magnetic vegetables and testiculars.

I pooshed the pooshbar. The door cracked open two eenches onto red-tinted darkness. Looking behind, I slipped through and let the door close very quietly behind me.

I stood on a landing with black steel stairs going up and down. The air in this stairwell was as cold as meat locker. The only light came from one weak lightbulb—a red lightbulb, the kind you use for developing photographical peektures. Everything in the stairwell stood bathed in bloody red glow.

I began to creep down the stairs, holding the cold metal railing.

The basement lay three long flights down. The farther down I went, the colder the air. I sheevered by the time I reached bottom.

The stairs ended at another door with a pooshbar. A red-painted sign hung on the door at my eyes level.

KEEP OUT!

I went through the door.

Another corridor with vents in ceiling poured down blasts of frigid air. This place was as cold as a morgue, maybe.

To my one side, another door. To my other side, all the way down, the entrance to the service elevator.

A hospital gurney sat before the service elevator, as if waiting to be taken away.

A body lay on the gurney, covered by a white sheet, as still as marble.

I had to know, Meero. I had to make certain this was not my father on the gurney. I moved toward it, at every moment expecting someone to burst in on me—Igor or Nurse Damantis or the doctor with those spidery eyes. My trembling hand reached for the sheet and ripped it back with one kveek motion, as a magician whips away a veil.

It was the screaming man from the third floor.

His mouth and eyes gaped wide open in terror. He was still screaming but in silence now. He was dead. He would scream in silence forever.

My brains wanted to explode out of the top of my head. I had to put my hand to my mouth to keep my own self from screaming.

No wonder that this basement was as cold as a morgue. It *was* a morgue. The frigid air kept the bodies cold.

Looking closer, I saw that there were no marks upon the screaming man. No blood. No sign of how he died. What had they done to him to keel him?

"They'll be coming any minute…"

"Yes, Doctor…"

The voices of Nurse Damantis and the doctor—and coming my way, too.

I did not have time to call the elevator or to run back to the stairwell. I stood there trapped in this corridor with this body and no place to go.

When you have no place, you must *make* place, Meero. This is exactly what I did.

I will tell you how in the next ladder.

Scrembling for my life,

Vospop

LADDER THIRTEEN
I Am Almost Died

Dear Meero,

I re-covered the body, crouched down, and kveekly sleed into the space below the sheet, by the gurney's wheels. A grid of metal bars gave me a sort of shelf that I could lie on. The sheet draped down almost to the floor and covered me.

Three sets of shoes came into view below the edge of the sheet: Igor's heavy work shoes, the doctor's pointy wing-tip shoes, and Nurse Damantis's spongy white soundless shoes.

"Has somebody been here?" the nurse's voice said.

"You're very nervous today," the doctor said.

"Ever since I found that boy upstairs . . ." the nurse said uneasily.

"Mindless drones," the doctor said in that moistureless voice. "I wouldn't worry about it. Igor, call the elevator. They'll be here in a moment."

The elevator shrieked and groaned somewhere upstairs as it began its slow descent. Who was this "they," Meero? Who was coming in a moment?

The nurse asked, "All went well in the Shock Chamber?"

My blood went ice as I heard the words. *The Shock Chamber.* What was that?

"All went perfectly," the doctor's voice said. "He frightened to death like a dream."

My heart began to pound so loudly I was afraid they would hear it drumming.

"I wish I could patent my Shock Chamber," the doctor said with a sigh. "Good, clean deaths with not a mark on the body. No injury to internal organs. Just a heart stopped by fear. I could make a fortune marketing and selling the chamber."

"Who would want to buy it?" the nurse said.

"Oh," the doctor said, "there are plenty of people. Gangsters. Dictators. Anybody who wants someone dead with no questions asked and no marks left on the *corpus*."

So they had someplace in this basement where they frightened their patients to death! But *why*, Meero? Why would anybody want to do such a thing?

The elevator arrived and shrieked. The folding gate rettled open. Igor pooshed the gurney (and me) into the elevator. The wheels went *squick, squick, squick, squick* even louder than before. I had added to the gurney's weight.

"Igor, do something about that wheel, will you?" the doctor said.

The folding gate rettled and clanged shut. We started upward.

Igor knelt down with a pocket oilcan to oil that squicky wheel. He bent so far, I could see his mouth and nose beneath the edge of the sheet. The tip of his tongue nestled in the corner of his mouth while he oiled. If he crouched one inch lower, he would see me!

"This fellow makes a superb corpse," the doctor continued.

"Yes," the nurse agreed. "Perfect for harvesting."

"God bless these Old World peasant constitutions and diets," the doctor said. "All natural and all organic. His lungs are absolutely magnificent. They'll go to that industrialist in Shanghai."

"What about his liver?" the nurse said.

"There's a banker in San Francisco waiting for that. His kidneys go to a film producer in Paris. We can parcel out every piece of him somewhere. I should think we can net about three million dollars from him, all told. Once he harvested fields. Now we harvest *him*. He'll soon be international! Cosmopolitan!"

Nurse Damantis chockled without humor.

So that was the secret, Meero. You disappeared into the Pilgrim's Paradise and they killed you without leaving a mark so that no vital organs would be ruined. This was why they weakened you first in a hospital bed. This was why they starved you. This was why they even let you hear the screams of the pipple on their way to death. It was all preparation. It was all to wear you down and get you ready for the Shock Chamber.

Who could I tell this to, Meero? Who would ever believe me?

And my father, Meero—my father was possibly headed for the Shock Chamber, too!

Unless I found him first.

Igor finished oiling the wheel. His face went away, the elevator shuddered to a stop, and Igor pooshed the gurney out. We had arrived back upstairs in the corridor that ran behind the kitchen. A car horn honked somewhere.

"There they are," the doctor said.

I felt a wave of fresh air as someone opened the door to the outside. Igor pooshed the gurney again, and through the metal bars I crouched upon I saw the dog turds and shards of glass of the alley. A car motor idled somewhere nearby.

"How are you, Doctor?" a man's voice said. I did not recognize this voice.

"Very well, thank you, Sergey."

"How are you, Nurse?" said Sergey. The nurse said nothing in reply.

The doctor said, "Louie, help us get this poor fellow into the hearse."

A soggy cigarette fell to the ground inches from my face. Another pair of shoes stepped up beside the gurney—the stained work shoes of the smogging security guard.

"Another one gone already." The doctor sighed, clicking his tongue with fake regret. "It's those immigrant diets that do it. All those fats. All that unhealthy living . . ."

So Louie the security guard with the soggy cigarettes was not in on the secret of the Pilgrim's Paradise.

I heard a trunk being opened and felt another wave of cold air. The "hearse" was a deep-freeze meat locker, too, designed to keep bodies fresh.

"Slide him out from under, Louie," the doctor said.

The sheet over the gurney shifted, then draped a few inches

lower. They had sleed the body out from underneath it into the back of the refrigeratored hearse.

"Nurse," the doctor said, "do you want to come along?"

"I'd like that," said Nurse Damantis's voice.

"Where should I put the gurney?" Igor asked.

"Put it," the doctor said, "in the chamber."

I could not help it, Meero. I let out a noise. I let out *eek* like trapped hamster, mostly!

But nobody heard me eeking because somebody slammed the back of the hearse just then.

The hearse pulled away, and Igor pooshed the gurney back inside and into the service elevator. Down we rode, back to the frigid air of the basement. More doors opening and closing. Dipper we went into the Pilgrim's Paradise. I wanted to dash out from under the gurney, but my legs would not obey me. My muscles had turned to mussels—the soft, cooked kind.

A different door opened, heavily, with a groan. Igor pooshed the gurney through it and the floor underneath me went from white tile to black tile. He stopped the gurney over the shining metal grill of a floor drain.

The heavy door groaned shut, taking all the light with it.

I was in the Shock Chamber.

Total darkly,

Vospop

LADDER FOURTEEN
I Find My Father, Dead or Alive

Dear Meero,

I waited before daring to do anything. A minute? Two minutes? Five minutes? Five seconds? In the dark, Meero, all clocks go crazy. So do your brains.

Finally I slipped out from my hiding place and creeped on all fours across the floor until I reached wall. I felt my way along this wall until I reached door. The door was made of thick steel plates, riveted togather.

There was no lock, only the rivets that held this door togather.

Was I locked in? Would I have to stay shut up in the dark of the Shock Chamber until somebody came and found me?

I set my shoulder to the door and laid the whole weight of my body against it.

Heavily, slowly, the door moved one eench. Igor had not secured it on the outside. I removed my beckpeck full of bricks and held it ready, like a sling. If Igor was outside, this beckpeck would make a fine weapon. I peered out the door.

Nobody outside. Igor had gone.

I found myself in a control room of some kind: machines and levers and knobs and screens. The control panel for shocking their patients to death.

I turned and looked back through the half-open door into the dimness of the Shock Chamber. The gurney sat in its center. The walls were rough, gray, bare stone. The floor was black, with that seeneester drain in the center. I did not know how they frightened their patients to death in the Shock Chamber. I did not want to know.

All this lay below the perfect surface of the Pilgrim's Paradise, Meero! This was the dark, hidden heart of things!

Something buzzed on the control panel. A red light started blinking.

I dropped my beckpeck and ran as fast as my feets would carry me. Through the door, into the cold corridor, back to the stairwell again. In the bloody-red darkness I raced up the three steep flights, panting and panicking, and plunged through the door to the first floor.

I found myself again standing in the corridor behind the kitchen. From the kitchen, I heard Mr. Stoodgly's cheerful tunes. From the Employee Dining Room, the *bipp, bipp, bipp* of Dood and Kyool's voodeo games. I felt as if I had been away for days.

I went into the Employee Dining Room and spun my baseball cap across the room. This woke Dood and Kyool from their voodeo trance.

"What's up, dood?" said Dood.

"Poot away your iPods and your mindiless games," I said. "Lend me your ears."

They stared at me, then at each other, then at me. Obediently they unplugged their heads. Perhaps I looked insane, Meero!

"This Pilgrim's Paradise we are in," I said, "is a death factory."

I then told them who I really was and why I was there. I told them of my father. I told them all that I had seen and heard that day. The screaming man, the gurney, the Shock Chamber. Their eyes grew as large as the screens on their voodeo games.

"So you mean," Dood said when I finished, "you mean you're here, like, *undercover?*"

"Yes," I said. "This I am meaning."

"You mean," Kyool said, "that Dr. Sarkoffagis is like some whoo-whoo mad scientist and he's got, like, a *torture chamber* downstairs?"

"This is exactly what I am meaning," I said. "And I tell you all this because I need your help. *Will* you help me?"

I looked from one to the other.

"Well, like . . . *sure!*" said Dood.

"You got it, man!" said Kyool. "Name it!"

I said, "First, we must find out if my father is still here."

"Was that a picture of your old man you showed us?" Dood asked. "Let's see it again."

I took out the peekture once more. They passed it back and forth.

"I dunno if I've seen him," Dood said.

Kyool said, "We could keep our eyes out when we pass out the supper boxes."

"So *we'd* be like undercover, too!"

"Kyool!"

"My friends," I said. "Thank you."

I shooked their hands heartily. They were not so used to hand-shaking. So we five-highed and banged our knuckles in friendship. This is American custom, Meero. Donut ask me why. Is quite painful.

"All for one," said Dood, "and one for I-forget-the-rest! How's it go?"

"All for one," I said, *"and one for all!"* And we five-highed and banged knuckles a few times more.

Mr. Stoodgly came in, clapping to rouse us.

"It's time, boys!" he said. "Let's get those suppers up there pronto! *Chop chop!*"

Dood and Kyool and I stood at attention and clicked our heels and saluted.

"Yes, *sir!*" we cried as one.

"That's the idea!" said Mr. Stoodgly, heading back out. "Team spirit! I love it!"

In two minutes Dood and Kyool had loaded up their wheelycarts and were ready to ascend. And with no bopping and wreegling, either! You see what a difference it makes, Meero, when you have a porpoise in life?

I was delivering the boxes on floor six when I heard running feetsteps in the corridor. It was Dood.

"Yo, Vospopper," he gasped, out of breath. " I think your old man's up on nine."

At Pilgrim's Paradise, the floors got worser the higher you went—the walls dimmer, the floors feelthier, the fluorescent lights more fleekery. The ninth floor, the top floor, was a tunnel out of hell. I swear I heard bats, Meero, rustling about in the darkness near the ceiling.

At room 903, I pooshed the door so hard, it almost knocked out Kyool, who was standing behind it.

My father lay in the bed. He turned his head and looked at me and cried *"Galoshkiss!"* and I bursted into tears.

What a scene was this, Meero! I fell upon him, wipping. Though he was strapped down, he was able to wrap his arms around me. And my father, my gloomy father, Meero, he wipped, too! He wipped, he laughed, he gave thanks to God.

It was full dramatic Slobovian scene, mostly!

The eyes of Dood and Kyool popped from their skulls at all this.

"Dood," said Dood, "I don't think *my* old man'd act like that."

"Mine neither," Kyool said. "Not even if I saved him from a mad scientist with a torture chamber."

"Poppup," I said, "we must get you out of here. And we must do it before the nurse and doctor return."

"There's no present like this time," my father quoted.

This was the happiest and least gloomiest proverb I had heard from him in very long time.

"You won't get him past Louie the security guard," Kyool said.

"Then I will take him out the *front* door," I said. "We will go down the elevator in the front of the building."

"O.K.," Dood said, "but we're goin' with you."

"We ain't stickin' around no death factory," Kyool said.

"Good," I said. "But you must kveekly finish passing out lunches to the patients. We cannot let these pipple starve. Meet me at the front elevator in five minutes."

They ran off to finish their boxes. Meanwhile, I sleed under the bed amongst years of rat turds and unlocked the straps that held my father down. My father's clothes were nowheres to be found. He would have to escape in the flimsy blue paper hospital gown and paper sleepers he was wearing.

He was able to walk if he leaned on my arm. As we reached the front elevator, Dood and Kyool joined us.

This was no shrieking, groaning cage but a smooth, quiet modern elevator. For the use of the doctor and the nurse, no doubtless. We all got in and I pressed floor one.

"Where do you think this elevator goes?" Dood said.

"Soon," I said, "we will find this out."

The doors sleed open at floor one and opened onto a small interior office. Beside a desk stood the two largest men I have ever seen. Just like whales, they were all neck. One whale was in blue suit, one whale was in brown. They had heads like buttox and fists the size of barbells.

"Galoshkiss!" said Dood and Kyool.

The whales charged us with their heads down.

I hit a floor button. Too late. The brown whale jammed the door open with his forearm. The blue whale grabbed me by the sweatshirt, ripped me out of the elevator, and flung me across the room, slamming me against a wall.

Well, Meero, this energized the undefeated Tree-Throwing Champion of Lower Slobovia. In an instant my father became the undefeated *Whale-Throwing Champion* of Lower Slobovia. He lifted the blue whale and threw him end-over-end-over-end across the room. The whale landed on his head, next to me, with a *thunk*.

The brown whale reached for a telephone on the desk. Too late! In one bound, my father was upon him and threw him too. My father threw him with a roar that made all the hairs on your body do The Wave, like at sports stadium!

When the brown whale landed, my father pulled him up and threw him again. Then he threw the blue whale again. Then he ripped out telephone from the wall and threw that. Then he threw the desk and chairs. He looked about for something else to throw.

"Poppup," I said, "enough throwing. We must go."

"Which way out?" my father roared. The blue whale made whimpering whale noises and pointed to a door. And out the door we ran.

Beyond that door lay the front lobby of the Pilgrim's Paradise. We found our way out of the first set of doors but could not find how to open the golden doors. Beyond their glass lay the street, and freedom.

"Boys," my father said, *"keek!"*

As one, Dood, Kyool, and I karate-kicked the golden doors and they too sleed open. It was hard to believe that these were the same two peemply pepperoni boys from Subway Sandwiches. I had learned a valuable lesson this day, Meero. I had learned that there is no anus who cannot be saved. You must only give an anus a porpoise in life.

Outside the golden doors, the day was settling down to a fine summery evening. Pipple went by us, not suspecting the adventures we had just been through. How odd to be standing in the sweet, open air, Meero. Like dream!

A taxicab screeched to a stop right before us.

"May I offer you gentlemen a ride?" the taxicab driver said. "Ohmygodyes?"

It was Mr. Awakan Singh, taxi number CO1935! More unbelievable!

"Be hopping in, please!" he said.

The two whales came running out into the street, waving their arms and cursing us. They chased the taxicab for half a block, but Mr. Singh was too fast. We were headed for home.

Breathing sigh from relief,

Vospop

LADDER FIFTEEN
How I Decided to Get into Dipper Trobble

Dear Meero,

At the apartment building Dood and Kyool helped me help my father up the stairs, along with Mr. Awakan Singh. As we had not enough moneys for taxicab fare, I had invited him in for a bite of Slobovian food.

When we walked into the apartment, there were more shouts, more wipping, more laughter but with more pipple this time. Grandma Aleenska wailed with happiness, dabbing a pair of fresh-peeled potatoes to her eyes. We all bursted into the Slobovian national anthem, "Don't Cry for Me, Slobovina," and we wipped some more. Even my uncle, sunk in the Armchair of Gloom, rose with shining eyes to embrace his lost brother and almost crushed him.

Mr. Awakan Singh was soon singing and dabbing his eyes with fresh-peeled potatoes, too. I could even swear I saw Dood and Kyool doing some dabbing.

Leena and Grandma Aleenska made a twelve-course Slobovian reunion meal. My father broke open a bottle of *vottsdott* for celebration. Meanwhile, I told all that I had seen and been through at the Pilgrim's Paradise that day. And what a day, Meero! Enough day for whole year!

When I had finished, Mr. Awakan Singh rose from his chair like a senator in a senatorium. "You must *do* something, Mr. Voss!" he said. "You cannot allow all those poor people to die!"

"Me?" I said. "Why me?"

All eyes were on me, Meero! Especially Leena's, which were brimming over with love and marriage. This was like combination of Pepto-Bismol and Ex-Lax to my guts.

Then the doorbell rang.

Everything stopped. The wipping stopped. The laughing stopped. The dabbing stopped. The drinking of *vottsdott* stopped. My first thought, Meero? I thought the two whales had come to get us.

Everybody turned and looked at *me* again.

"Answer it, Vospop," Leena veespered. Even Leena was frightened. Leena Aleenska! Frightened, Meero!

"Why me?" I said. "You're bigger and stronger than I am."

"Answer!" she hissed.

I did as she hissed. I opened the door.

Who stood outside but your twin cousins Lilka and Lilka!

Well, Meero. More embracing, more wipping, more laughing, more shouting, more pipple falling into other pipple's arms! More pipple dabbing more eyes with more potatoes. More Slobovian-style emotions. More *vottsdott*. Uncle Shpoont was so moved, he rearranged all the furniture, in the old Slobovian tradition, to mark change.

Dood shooked his head in wonder.

"You know, dood," he said to me, "you Slobovians are one crazy people!"

Leena and Grandma Aleenska made a second twelve-course Slobovian reunion meal. While we ate it, Lilka and Lilka related how they had smoggled themselves to America through third-class mail.

Dood and Kyool had never seen anything like these girls in flowered peeg-iron dresses and shoes like shoe boxes and hair like helmets. But they could not converse because Dood and Kyool spoke no Slobovian except *"galoshkiss."* Lilka and Lilka spoke no Eenglish except the words "Speak-and-Span."

Kyool veespered to me, "Voss, these girls are built like fire hydrants!"

I veespered back, "Is the Slobovian way. I'm sorry."

"Sorry?" he said. "I think they're kinda *hot,* man!"

"I think so, too," said Dood. "Only how do you tell 'em apart? They're even *named* the same!"

"Of course," I said. "They are twins. Lilka is the lyrical one. Lilka is the beautiful one."

"How can you tell which Lilka's lyrical and which Lilka's beautiful," Dood said, "when they look totally identical?"

"This," I said, "is great Slobovian reedle."

It was midnight by the time we finished the two twelve-course Slobovian meals. Dood and Kyool went home, driven by Mr. Awakan Singh. First, however, Mr. Singh got the recipe for curried brains from Grandma Aleenska.

"I will curry some brains immediately I go home!" he cried. "I will curry some brains for my sister! *Ohmygodyes!*"

My uncle, however, had slumped back into the Armchair of Gloom. I knelt beside him.

"Forgive me, Uncle," I said, "for what I said to you."

He shooked his head.

"No, Vospop," he said. "You spoke me truth. You told me I own nothing. I must only learn how to live with the truth. I must learn how to live with nothing."

"No man can live twenty-four hours a day with nothing but the truth," I said. "He needs vacation!"

"This"—he shrugged—"is my problem, Vospop, not yours. Good night and God bless you. You have greatness in you, nephew. Worry about it."

It was now two o'clock in the morning and all had settled themselves to slipp, yet I was not tired. I creeped out the front door and went downstairs and sat on the stoop.

The street was empty. No pipple. No traffic. Only the changing, cleeking green-red-green of the traffic lights at the corner.

Meanwhile, my brains cleeked, too, churning the events of the day. My brains took them in like pork into a sausage grinder while adding the garlic of my own reflections. My father was home and I was safe. I would never have to go back to Pilgrim's Paradise again.

But was I really so safe, Meero?

No.

First, if I did not convince Leena Aleenska to marry Stepin N. Klozdadorski, I was (as we say in Slobovian) *dedmeetski*.

Second, at the Pilgrim's Paradise they must have realized by now that my father was gone. The two whales had seen our faces as we took him. I also knew about the Shock Chamber. The nurse and the doctor would know I knew because they would find my beckpeck down in the basement. They would not want me roaming this city with their dirty secrets.

Did Nurse Damantis and the doctor have any way to trace me?

What would they do if they did track me down?

Third, Mr. Awakan Singh's words played over and over in my brains.

"You must do something, Mr. Voss . . . You cannot allow all those poor people to die . . .!"

How could I leave Erica Mannska in the Pilgrim's Paradise after swearing I would help her? How could I abandon her to the Shock Chamber and a refrigerated hearse? How could I abandon all those pipple to such a fate?

A voice interrupted my thoughts.

"Bushweck, Vospop."

A young woman stood before me at the bottom of the stoop. She wore the traditional Slobovian costume—the flowered peeg-iron dress, the helmet hair, the shoe box shoes. I did not recognize her, though she gazed at me as if she knew me. Unlike most Slobovian women, her helmet of hair was golden color. Also, she had no eyebrows to speak of and no sideburns. She was not built like fire hydrant but like ironing board. She was so thin, the flowered peeg-iron dress hung on her like a bedsheet draped over a kitchen chair.

"*Tiffany!*" I cried. "What is happened? Is that you inside that?"

Her lower leep began to tremble. Her leeps were no longer crimson with God-by-Tiffany leepstick.

"You mean . . ." she said with tears in her eyes, "you don't, like, *like* me like this? I thought maybe if I looked like this, you'd like me again. If I looked like . . . like *her*."

She could not speak Leena's name. She took out an enormous checkered Slobovian handkerchief the size of a hand towel and wipped into it.

"But Tiffany," I said, "these clothings are a lie! You are not Slobovian! You are spoiled reetch girl!"

"But this is America," she whined. "In America you can be anything you want. Especially if you're rich."

"You can impersonate Slobovian girl, but you cannot *be* Slobovian girl."

"I can't?"

"No!"

"Oh, Voss," she said. "I've missed you so much!"

"Is only one day since I saw you," I said.

"I know, but you've, like, totally *ruined* me! I didn't even want to *brunch* today! I'm a brunching *person*, Voss. Who *am* I if I'm not brunching?"

"Go home, Tiffany," I said.

She sighed and took out her platinum celephone and punched in some numbers.

"Carlo?" she said to her celephone.

Her gold limousine pulled up. Carlo stepped out and opened the door for her. Tiffany got wippful again and dabbed the hand towel to her nose.

"*Beckwash*, Vospop," she said.

"*Beckwash*, Tiffany," I said. She got in and rode away.

Once again I did not slipp so much that night. When I did fall aslipp, I dreamt of Mr. Stoodgly chasing me down a long, dark corridor with a rusty butcher knife and saying, "*Chop chop! Chop chop!*" This was very unpleasant. Even in the dream I wished for another dream, with Leena's clean spatula instead.

Exhausted from dreams,

Vospop

LADDER SIXTEEN
More Crazy Plans

Dear Meero,

I woke and dressed before dawn. Leena found me in the kitchen finishing a cup of coffee.

"Do you have a plan, Vospop?"

"I do," I said.

"Good," she said. "I thought so."

"The plan is impossible," I said. "It's mad. It's insane."

"All the better," she said. "You will be praised more when you accomplish it."

But when I went downstairs, Noah McBloomingdale stood waiting for me in the street. He stood before a purring gold limousine with tinted windows.

"Howdy, Voss," said Mr. McBloomingdale. "Have you got a minute for a fond and foolish old man?"

He humbly took off his cowboy hat and showed his noble head. From the purple baggages under his eyes, I guessed that he too had not slipped so much this night.

In truth, I did not have a minute. Yet I did not want to say no. Is a terrible thing to be brought up polite, Meero. Donut do it!

He looked down at the cowboy hat in his hand and turned it like a wheel.

"Coupla thayngs," he began. "First off, yer uncle. Now, I called him on the phone a multitude o' times yesterday. But he won't talk to me. He refuses to come to the phone even to say howdy do. And I've gotten real fond of yer uncle, Voss. *Real* fond."

"My uncle is not very well right now," I said.

"Well, if there's anything I can do," he said with energy, "I'll do it. I'll fly him to the finest doctor in the world in my private jet!"

"He is not that kind of not well," I said. "This is gloom."

"I see," he said. "Well, the thayng is, Voss, yer uncle gave me some real good advice. The man's a dang financial genius! Past coupla days, he's made me a fortune for my charities. If you could just get him to utter the word *buy* or *sell,* I'd be much obliged to you. I don't mean to put this all on money. Don't fergit, I'm a philantherpissed. I deal in ideals. But y'see, yer uncle's got my investments so tied up in knots, he's the only one can unravel 'em!

"Now the other thayng, Voss . . ."

He cleared his throat uneasily.

"The other thayng is Tiffany. I know you and Tiff had a tiff. She's had a multitude o' tiffs with a multitude o' men in her short time. But this time it's different. She's a-mopin' 'round all day lookin' more hangdog than a drowned puppy. She ain't goin' out in the helicopter. She ain't brunchin'. Plus, she's wearin' the craziest getup you ever seen. This flowered dress, it looks like it's made outa pig iron. And she's wearin' these shoes that look like forty-pound weights."

"Yes," I said. "She is impersonating a Slobovian. She is try-ing to impress me."

"A Slobovian? Wait a minute . . . You mean . . .?"

His hand stopped rotating his cowboy hat and his eyes grew wide.

"Voss, you don't mean to tell me . . . You don't mean y'er a *Slobovian?*"

"Yes," I said, "that is what I am meaning. I am fool-blood, pedigreed, 52nd generation Slobovian. This is as far back as we go. After that is only cavemen."

"So y'er not *British?*"

He made a low whistle and shooked his head. Maybe he even backed away a step.

"Whoo!" he breathed. "Slobovian, huh. That's serious stuff, Voss. You know what Slobovian means in this country. It ain't the lowest of the low. It's *below* the lowest of the low. But listen, I'm open-minded. We all came here from some-where and I got charity in my heart as well as in my pockets! And I love my daughter. So I'm willin' to overlook yer Slobo-vitude. All I ask is this: Make nice to Tiffany, will ya? You've broke her dang *heart*, Voss!"

This was when I had a breelliant idea, Meero!

"Mr. McBloomingdale," I said, "let me make you an offer."

This word perked him up instantly. The cowboy hat began spinning like Wheel of Fortune.

"An *offer?*" he said. "Now y'er talkin'! Offers are somethin' I know about. So go right ahead, Voss. Hit me with anything!

Negotiate! *Bargain at me!* But just remember: y'er dealin' with an *expert.* And don't say later I didn't warn ya."

"There is a man named Bilias Opchuck," I said, "to whom I owe one hundred thousand dollars for some Chiss Poffs. I have until midnight tonight before Bilias Opchuck cores me like an apple because of these Chiss Poffs."

"What in tarnation is a *Chiss Poff?*"

"Is too complicated."

"Say, wait a minute. Is this fella the blackmarketeer and smuggler?"

"How do you know Bilias Opchuck?" I said.

"Big money's big money whether it's charities, factories, or thieveries, Voss," he said. "We're all of us thicker'n thieves! Some of us *are* thieves! So what's yer offer?"

"I will make nice to your daughter and squire her around town again. I will also talk her out of her Slobovian costume."

"If . . .?"

"If you pay Bilias Opchuck the one hundred thousand dollars."

"Hunderd thousand dollars . . ." he muttered. "Hmmm . . ." He scratched his chin.

"Or the equivalent," I said, "in Chiss Poffs."

He said, "I don't deal in Chiss Poffs, Voss. Not until they're recognized as a world currency. God knows it might happen, but it ain't happened yet. Let's get back to this hunderd thousand."

"What is one hundred thousand dollars," I said, "compared to all the billions my uncle has gained you?"

"It's still a hunderd thousand dollars, that's what it is. And that's a lotta pesos, amigo. But remember: I'm *negotiatin'* now. I'm usin' all my crafty tactics. So lemme make you a counteroffer. I will pay this fella Upchuck in cash or Chiss Poffs or however else he wants it—but you gotta promise to marry my darlin' daughter someday."

"*Galoshkiss!*" I said.

"It's the only way you can mend her busted heart."

"But I am only fifteen!" I said.

"That's O.K.," he said. "I'll take a rain check. Let's say you marry her when y'er twenty-one. I can wait. But believe you me, son, on yer 21st birthday I'll be there, knockin' on yer door and callin' in my debt. And I *always* call in my debts!!"

"But," I said. "But . . ."

"But me no but's," he said. "What's yer answer? Do you wanna get married to a multibillionairess, or do you want to get cored and pitted like a winesap apple? What's the verdict? Promise or no promise?"

I took deep gulp, Meero. It was like swallowing my whole brains down my throat. What could I did, Meero?

"All right," I said. "I promise."

"*Deal!*" he cried. He stuck out his hand, and I shooked it, or rather it shooked me. Then he flung his hat into the air.

"*Whoo-EEE! Yippeeeeeeee! Yippie ai oh kai ay! Whoop whoop whoop! Hot dawg! Hot dangit, hot dawgit, hot diggety DAWG!*"

The back door of the limousine flew open and Tiffany popped out. She threw herself into my arms.

"Oh, Voss, I'm so happy! I'm, like, so *stoked!* I'm gonna start planning the wedding, like, *today!* This is so *cool!* I can't wait to go to brunch and call all my friends!"

"Congratulations, son!" Mr. McBloomingdale said. "You just got yerself a trophy wife!"

Tiffany looked down at her flowered dress and shoe box shoes as if seeing them for first time.

"*EEEEEEUWWWWWW!*" she said. "What am I doing in these *clothes?* I gotta go shopping."

"Looks like a full cure to me, Voss!" Mr. McBloomingdale said.

He leaned over close to me and dug his elbow into my ribs.

"*I'll owe you a big one fer this,*" he veespered. "*You call in the debt any old time, pardner.* C'mon, Tiff, the man's got some urgent business to tend to. Let's let him tend it. So long, Voss! See ya 'round the ranch!"

He yippeed and yahood a few more times. Shades snepped up and pipple looked out of windows all up and down the street. He and Tiffany got into the limousine and drove away.

Now I was not only fated, I was *engaged* to be married, no matter what. And to the wrong person!

What would Leena say?

"*You traitor!*" a voice called out.

Leena was leaning out the window over my head.

"We are *still* fated, Vospop Vsklzwczdztwczky!" she cried. "You cannot change this fate, no matter what!"

She slammed the window. As she did so, the sun came up down the street and slapped me in the face.

As always at such moments, Meero, I took my pocket watch from my trousers pocket, but it did not tell me the time. It only told me the moment at which I had broken Leena Aleenska's heart.

So many events already and the day was just begun! America, you never close!

And now I was going to be Tiffany McBloomingdale's miserable husband.

Miserably,

Vospop

LADDER SEVENTEEN
The Gathering of the Slobovians

Dear Meero,

I still had my insane plan for the pipple of Pilgrim's Paradise to poot into motion. So I started away up the street. But before I had gone ten paces, I was interrupted again.

"*Yo, Voss,*" a voice cried. "*Wait up!*"

It was Dood and Kyool running after me.

"Where ya goin'?" Dood panted as they caught me.

"Can we come, too?" said Kyool.

I said, "What are you two doing here?"

"We got nothin' better to do," Dood said. "I mean, we're out of a job at the Paradise."

"Plus," Kyool said, "things are always, like, *hoppin'* around you, man. You're like a one-man action movie."

"Plus," Dood said, "we thought maybe we could hang out a little with your twin friends. I spent the whole night thinkin' about Lilka."

Kyool said, "And I spent the whole night thinkin' about *Lilka.*"

"Is this why you two are so dressed up?" I said. "I hardly recognize you."

They looked embareassed. They now wore button-down blue shirts and chinos that fit them and polished leather shoes. Kyool had tucked his dreadlocks into a knitted wool cap that matched his shirt. They looked like two other pipple entirely!

"Yeah," Dood admeeted. "I mean, we looked at each other last night and said, *Hey! We're dressed like a coupla anuses!*"

Kyool said, "But hey, Voss man, is Leena, like, your girl-friend? Is it true you're gonna marry her sometime?"

"She's pretty kyool," Dood said.

"I just got engaged . . ." I said.

They fell all over me, patting me on the beck and five-highing me and banging knuckles.

". . . to Tiffany McBloomingdale," I added.

"*HUH?!*" they said.

"Whoa!"

"Whoo . . ."

"Wow . . ."

"Leena's gonna kick your butt, man."

"I mean, you and Leena are, like, *fated,* dood! You can't do nothin' about *fate*! You sure can't *change* fate!"

"Is complicated story," I said. "At moment, I have urgent beeznest. You want to come? There is no time to be losed."

Again I went my way. They pressed close, keeping step, eager to see what new adventure I was headed for or what fresh trobble.

The street was coming alive now—as alive as the illegal Slobovian section ever came. The stoops were filling up with slouching, silent, disheveled men and women. Slobovian shopkippers were opening their sad shops and pooshcarts as if they expected no customers. Children lounged on front steps in deep deep-pression instead of running about. A few Slobovians even begged pennies here and there on street corners.

The address I was looking for turned out to be a decrappit building that sagged as if weary of trying to stand up straight. The bricks themselves looked crushed from holding up the other bricks, and the windows were winking shut by force of gravity.

A drunkard sprawled across the front steps, an empty *vottsdott* bottle in his hand.

"*Bushweck*, brother," I said. "I am looking for Tomas Mannsky."

"He just got home with a new set of hubcaps," the drunkard drawled in a blurry drunken voice. "Fourth floor."

I went in, followed by Dood and Kyool. As we ascended, we passed a few pipple coming down the twisted, narrow slum staircase. I said, *"Bushweck."* They shouldered past me without a word. The Slobovian pipple had come to this, Meero. They passed a fellow Slobovian without a greeting!

A door stood open on the fourth floor, looking into a tiny kitchen. I knew this was Tomas Mannsky's flat because the kitchen was filled with hubcaps. The chrome disks were stacked up like enormous, unusable coins in a dream. A man with black rings around his eyes wearily piled up a new stack in a corner. This, I knew, must be Tomas Mannsky. He was a small, sturdy man with the strong, delicate hands of a metalworker.

I knocked. He looked at me. He looked at Dood and Kyool. He went back to stacking hubcaps. To this, too, the Slobovian pipple had descended, Meero. He did not ask me to sit down, he did not put out food or drink, he did not offer to lend me money at no interest.

"Tomas Mannsky," I said, "I bring a message from your wife."

He dropped the hubcaps, which fell about his feet like the breelliant scales from some giant's eyes.

"My wife . . .?" he said, staring at me.

"From Erica," I nodded. "You took her to Pilgrim's Paradise?"

He nodded, mute.

I said, "When you went back, they told you she wasn't there?"

"You have seen her?" he said. He had tears in his voice. "You have talked to Erica? She's *alive*? Thank God!"

"Here is her message to you," I said. *"Help me."*

"How?" he said. "Anything! I will do anything, just tell me, plizz!"

"I have plan," I said.

"Is it impossible?"

"Yes."

"Is it mad? Is it insane? Is it Slobovian?"

"Yes," I said. "But we cannot accomplish it ourselves. You are a thief, no? And you know other thieves?"

He nodded.

"Good," I said. "You and your fellow thieves will come in handy."

Kveekly I told him what he had to do. He nodded at everything I said. With every nod you saw a new wave of energy surge through him, straightening him, erasing the black targets from around his eyes.

"Yes!" he cried when I had finished. "I will do it!"

He pulled out a chair for each of us.

"Sit down, gentlemen!" he said. "Can I offer you something to itt? Something to drink? Can I lend you some money at no interest that you never need to pay back?"

Now he was Slobovian!

"Thank you, Tomas Mannsky," I said, "but there is no time for that. Now listen. For this plan to happen, everyone must gather no later than noon."

"Done!" he said, thumping the table. "Where shall we gather?"

"Maybe one of the Slobovian churches. We need a place that will fit a lot of pipple."

"The Church of Saint Anesthesia," he suggested. "That's the biggest."

"Good," I said. "Now you pass the word and so will we."

We all shooked hands and I started out with Dood and Kyool.

"Wait!" Tomas Mannsky said. "What should I tell everyone?"

"Tell them," I said, "that a fellow Slobovian—no, tell them

that a *fellow human being* needs their help. Needs *Slobovian* help. If you tell them that, they will come."

I started out again. Again he stopped me.

"Wait!" he cried, grabbing my sleeve from behind. "Who are you? *What* are you? Are you an angel from heaven?"

"No," I said. "I am seemply Vospop Vsklzwczdztwczky."

All morning Dood and Kyool and I walked from doors to doors, floors to floors, buildings to buildings, talking to illegal Slobovians in doorways, ringing doorbells, knocking at flats, going into shops and speaking to shopkippers, but most importantly passing the word to beggars on the street, for a beggar in his time meets everybody.

The word spread kveekly and soon preceded us. By midmorning, pipple knew why we had come and invited us in, offering us food and drink and money at no interest. Every avenue was full of pipple talking excitedly. From window to window and doorway to doorway they spoke, out-of-work illegal Slobovians who had not exchanged a word in weeks or months or years.

At noon, pipple swarmed the street before the Church of Saint Anesthesia. They crowded the front doors and thronged past the wondering face of Pastor Schlongo, who had not seen such congregation in years. They filled the pews all the way to the edges of the church and into the side chapels. More pipple spilled into the aisles and jammed the space at the back. When all the places downstairs were packed, they crowded the choir loft.

I stood in the sanctuary next to Tomas Mannsky, watching the last pipple enter. Painted scenes from the life of Saint Anesthesia adorned the church walls around me. Here was Saint Anesthesia preaching to the dentists in the teeth of adversity. Here was Saint Anesthesia converting the oral hygienists though standing within the very jaws of death. These scenes filled me hope and courage, Meero. Is that not the porpoise of saints?

The bells in the tower rang out twelve o'clock. When the last chime sounded, Tomas Mannsky pressed my arm.

"*Korset,* Vospop," he veespered, wishing me courage in the ancient Slobovian way. For the word *korset,* as you know, means *"Gird your loins. And if not yours, then somebody else's."*

I ascended the spiral stairs of the marble pulpit and took my place at the lectern. It was like standing in the prow of a great sheep before a sea of knobbly, complicated Slobovian faces. You never saw so many flowered peeg-iron dresses or smelled so much Vitalis hair oil. My father and my uncle and Leena and Grandma Aleenska sat in the front pew. Dood and Kyool sat behind them in the second pew with Lilka and Lilka. Behind them sat Mr. Awakan Singh with his clarinetist sister, Singh-Singh Singh.

"*Bushweck, Slobóviki!*" I greeted everyone.

As one, the congregation responded in chorus, calling me brother:

"*Bushweck, brewski!*"

As we had no time to be losed, I kveekly related my experiences in the Pilgrim's Paradise. I told about my father's narrow escape and about the narrow escape of his all-organic, all-natural Slobovian organs. I spoke of Erica Mannska, who was still trapped in the Pilgrim's Paradise and probably marked for death.

Even before I finished, a man jumped to his feet in the center of the church's nave.

"We must storm this place and save Erica Mannska!" he cried. "She is a Slobovian!"

A roar of approval followed his words.

"*No!*" I shot back. "She is a human being! As are all the prisoners of Pilgrim's Paradise, whatever their nation! And we cannot storm the place, for the police will be called. We will be arrested for trespassing and deported, one and all. I have another idea!"

The crowd hung on my next words in silence.

"*We must rescue them all!*" I said.

Instantly, Meero (for Slobovians are big of heart if small of wallet), a deafening roar of approval greeted my words.

A woman shouted, "How will we get them all out?"

"We will *steal* them," I said. "Are many of us not reduced to thievery and smoggling? Have poverty and prejudice not turned honest, illegal Slobovians into master burglars? Let us use the talents we have learned in America! I say we *smoggle* these poor pipple out!"

"*Hallelujah!*" they cried, which in Eenglish is "*Hurrah!*"

"Every afternoon," I said, "a black truck arrives at the back door of Pilgrim's Paradise delivering so-called food to the inmates. Here is my plan. We will bring in a truck of our own—

a whole fleet of trucks—and overcome the guard at the back door. Into these trucks we will load the patients and smoggle them away. But we will need the help of every Slobovian man and boy to do this."

Grandma Aleenska shot to her feet in the front pew.

"*And* every Slobovian woman and girl!" she shouted.

"Yes!" cried Leena Aleenska, rising, too. "Must we only cook and bake and iron and clean? This is America, where woman can be thieves and smogglers, too!"

As one, the women and girls of the congregation rose to their feet and shooked their fists and stamped their shoe box shoes, calling their sisters to arms. The stamping was like cannon thunder.

"Good!" I said. "But we will need a diversion at the front door of Pilgrim's Paradise to distract the nurse and the doctor and their accomplice, Igor, while we snick the inmates out the back. Who will volunteer for this? And let me warn you: This is a dangerous mission!"

"*I will do it!*" a voice cried.

My Uncle Shpoont shot to his feet.

"No, Uncle!" I said.

"Yes, Nephew!" he said. "We know that this nurse and this doctor like Slobovians for our excellent all-organic and all-natural organs. I am the finest organs you can offer! And what better man to distract these villains than someone who has been distracted in his time? Besides, I was once the greatest Shiksepeerean actor in all Slobovia! Who can fool them better than I? I can give them a deathbed scene that will distract them even if you stole the whole building out from under them!"

He raised his index finger dramatically to show what a powerful actor he was. Everyone gasped as he did so. Then everyone applauded. He was breelliant, Meero!

"I will do this to regain my honor," he said. "For I have been a deluded fool who thought he owned the whole world— and who lost the world by thinking that."

"But the nurse has seen you already," I protested. "She knows your face."

"Not," he said, "if I *shave off my mustache!*"

A cry of horror filled the church. My uncle's mustache was justly famous. (And as you know, the mustache is the national flower of Slobovia.) To shave off such a fixture would be like shaving the Eiffel Tower off Paris.

My uncle held out a hand to quiet the crowd. "Yes," he said. "I will sacrifice even my mustache for this mission!"

"But to shave off such a luxurious growth," I protested, "could take hours!"

"*No!*" said another voice.

All heads whipped around to see who this was. A tiny man with a shiny and hairless face had risen.

He said, "My name is Massimo Meeshky. Before I became a Slobovian jewel thief, I was Upper Slobovia's greatest barber. I still carry my barber tools with me everywhere!"

He produced an old, carved wooden box and flipped it open.

This revealed a glittering set of scissors and razors and combs, laid within the velvet interior like a set of duelling pistols.

Massimo Meeshky said, "I can shave off your uncle's mustache *in one minute!*"

"Very well," I agreed. "All we need now are the trucks to do the smoggling."

"*One moment!*" a harsh voice called out from the very back.

The crowd in the center aisle parted and a man stepped forward. He wore a long black trench coat and removed his gray fedora hat to reveal a head shaped like a ham.

It was Bilias Opchuck.

A murmur ran through the crowd like wind passing over wheat. "*Bilias Opchuck . . .! Bilias Opchuck . . .!*"

"How do you do, mostly," he growled. "Yes! I am Bilias Opchuck, and nobody smoggles nothing without me! I also have a whole fleet of black trucks *designed* for smoggling! My trucks will look exactly like Pilgrim's Paradise food-delivery truck—because *I* am the man who sells Pilgrim's Paradise its food! Is all stolen, of course."

Now I knew why that ancient cake in the lunch box had looked so familiar. It was one of Bilias Opchuck's stolen stollen.

"Fear not, then, *Slobóviki,*" he said. "*I* will provide the trucks!"

Well, the stained glass in the church *rettled* as the crowd shouted, "*Hallelujah!*" again. But then Bilias Opchuck raised his hand and with fury in his face he pointed a warning finger at me.

"But donut tink, Vospop Vsklzwczdztwczky," he growled, "that you get off so easy!"

My knees turned to vanilla pooding, Meero. "But Mr. Noah McBloomingdale will pay you for the Chiss Poffs . . ." I protested.

"He *has* paid me," he said. "One hundred thousand dollars. But there is also the matter of my illegitimate son, Stepin N. Klozdadorski. You have broken his heart, Vospop Vsklzwczdztwczky. So I will *still* meet you at midnight for our appointment, no matter what. Just tink of a *cored apple!*"

The place buzzed as everyone wondered what meant this midnight apple. I could feel Leena looking at me queazically, for of course she knew nothing about this.

"Tonight at midnight," Bilias Opchuck roared at me. *"Curtains!"*

He turned and stalked out of the church.

"Pay no attention," I cried, "to the man who just said *curtains.* This is a private matter betwin me and him! And we have pipple to save from the Pilgrim's Paradise!"

My father rose with a question.

"Vospop," he said, "what will we do with all these pipple after we smoggle them?"

"We are Slobovians, Poppup," I said. "Is this not our answer? I ask you, what *must* we do with them?"

"Welcome them!" he cried.

The Gathering of the Slobovians

"Hide them!" cried someone else.

"Take them into our homes until they can return to theirs!" cried another someone else.

"Feed them seven-course Slobovian meals to nurse them back to health!" said a third somebody.

"A perfect Slobovian answer," I said. "Now there is no time to be losed! Let's begin!"

Rushing into street,

Vospop

LADDER EIGHTEEN
The Big Smoggle

Dear Meero,

Within minutes, a fleet of black trucks chauffeured by Bilias Opchuck's hired thieves lined up at the curb outside the church. I took a seat high up in the cab of the first truck alongside my father. He looked ready to throw anything in his path—animal, vegetable, or criminal. He squeezed my knee in his powerful grip.

"Ah, Vospop," he sighed. *"Is good to be alive!"*

My father was shedding gloom like dog sheds hair in springtime.

The congregation poured out of the church and into the backs of the trucks. Even Pastor Schlongo joined us in his black, flepping cassock. The last to leave the church was a man who looked familiar but I did not recognize. He lifted his gray fedora hat and waved it at me.

"What do you tink, nephew?" he called out. "Am I disguised in my nakedness?"

It was Uncle Shpoont, minus mustache, Meero. Massimo Meeshky had shaved his mustache in the baptismal font with five strokes of his glittering razor!

Uncle Shpoont climbed into Mr. Awakan Singh's taxicab, which was to lead the way. When my uncle's hand waved from a window, the trucks' engines roared to life and we all headed for the Pilgrim's Paradise.

When we pulled into the alley behind the building, I saw Louie the security guard leaning up against the wall as always, a soggy cigarette smoldering between his leeps. He barely glanced at us when we pulled up before the kitchen door. But when he saw me descend from the cab, he straightened up and fleeked his limp cigarette away.

Then he saw my father descend—my father, who in one day seemed to have gained five inches in height. My father threw himself on the man and lifted Louie for throwing among the dog turds.

"*Galoshkiss!*" Louie cried out.

My father hesitated.

"*Galoshkiss?*" my father said, and lowered Louie to eyes level. "You are Slobovian?"

"Am I Slobovian?" the guard said. "Fifty-two generations! I am actually a concert pianist but could find no work here in America as concert pianist so I became security guard in an alley fool of dog turds! My true name is Luka Vsklzwczdztwczky."

"But *our* name is Vsklzwczdztwczky!" my father said.

The two men stared at each other.

"*BREWSKI!*" they cried, greeting itch other as brother Slobovians.

"*KEESHKI!*" they cried, greeting itch other as cousins.

Then they bounced each other up and down a few times.

"Poppup," I said, "enough bouncing! We have no time to be losed."

Kveekly my father told Luka Vsklzwczdztwczky why we were there and what we intended. Luka was shocked to hear the goings-on inside the Pilgrim's Paradise, of which he was innocent. His response was immediate.

"I am yours!" he said.

My father set his fingers to his leeps and let out a piercing whistle. Our fleet of trucks rolled into view, roaring into the alley. The backs of the trucks opened and an army of Slobovian men, women, boys, girls, and one priest spilled out.

"This way!" I called to them. I threw open the kitchen door. With Tomas Mannsky in the lead, our army streamed inside. Some headed for the service elevator. Others made for the stairwell. Grandma Aleenska passed me and Leena, too, then Dood and Kyool with Lilka and Lilka. The crowd was too thick for the narrow door.

"There is another way in!" Luka called out. "Follow me!"

He led another part of the company toward a freight entrance farther down the alley.

When the last person disappeared inside, I stepped into the dark, silent, cavern-like kitchen of the Pilgrim's Paradise. The lights still fleekered, the ceiling still dripped, the brown beetle still did his laps in the soup. After all that commotion outside, the quiet was crippy.

"What are you doing here?" a voice said behind me.

I turned around. The lights fleekered up.

"Mr. Stoodgly . . .!" I said. I had completely forgotten all about him! He stood now in the doorway of his office. But he was not the cheeriful seempleton I had known before. That pink and cheerful patsy face had changed into a stiff, pale mask of narrow-eyed hatred.

"I asked you," he said in a low voice, "what you're doing here."

A peestol appeared in his hand.

"Put your hands over your head," he said. "Chop chop."

Just then we heard a noise from the corridor behind the kitchen. Voices and feetsteps. They were bringing down the first patients from the upper floors.

"Get them into the truck!" a voice called.

Mr. Stoodgly must have realized what was happening. He ran into his office and reached for the telephone. In a moment, he would be speaking to Nurse Damantis.

In one motion I grabbed a rusting cast-iron skillet from the crusted stove and frisbeed it fifty feet, straight through the door of Mr. Stoodgly's office. The skillet caught him square in the meedle of the chest, flinging him backward. The peestol flew from his hand and stuck to the magnetic food chart on the wall, firing as it landed and blasting a hole in the ceiling.

Mr. Pat Stoodgly did not know that I am undefeated Cast-Iron-Skillet-Throwing Champion of Lower Slobovia.

He righted himself and lunged for the telephone.

Now I flung an omelet pan that sliced through the telephone wire. I then whipped a heavy metal pie pan that broke Mr. Stoodgly's nose and laid him flat in his office. With the telephone wire I tied his hands and feets, just as pipple do in American movies. (You see, Meero? America is nothing but movies all day long!)

Meanwhile, this is what was happening at the front of the building. I give you my Uncle Shpoont's own words, which he told me later:

"I was magnificent, Vospop!" he said. "Mr. Awakan Singh's taxicab pulled up before the Pilgrim's Paradise. I stumbled from the cab, grabbing my chest and collapsing amongst the flower beds with spectacular heart attack. I choked! I gasped! I gagged! I turned blue! My hands scrabbled the air as if grasping for breath!

"Miss Singh thew herself to her knees and wept and she wailed, begging all passersby for help and screaming for aid.

"This was a masterstroke, Vospop! For what Pilgrim's Paradise did *not* want was too many public attentions.

"So what happens then? The golden doors slide open and Igor comes out to get us. So eager were they to get us off their street!

"Igor helped me to my feet and urged me inside. I started for the golden doors with Igor to one side of me, Miss Singh to the other. I dragged my feet. I gasped for air. I stopped and shooked my head, protesting that I was too weak.

"As we reached the golden doors, I heard in the distance your father's whistle. By this whistle I knew that you had gotten in the back door.

"Slowly, slowly, we entered the golden doors. I not only dragged my feet. I walked on my knees. I was in slow motion, Vospop. I was so slow I looked like nature program on television!

"Then the dark doors opened and the nurse appeared. She was as cool as November, Vospop. And with eyes like a death ray!

"'*Can I help you?*' she said.

"'*I am poor penniless Slobovian!*' I cried, rising to my knees. '*Help me, plizz!*'

"The moment I said 'Slobovian,' I saw how eenterested she was. I saw her greed for my healthy Slobovian organs.

"'*My name,*' I said, '*is Gogol Gszmktpwskczczcztkp . . .*'

"The saying of this name alone took me two minutes, Vospop.

"'*. . . szmktpwskczczcztktpwskczpky.*'

"I coughed. I sneezed. I wheezed. I hacked. I flushed. I got dizzy. My teeth chattered. My nose dribbled. My ears filled up with wax. I was the whole medical dictionary of symptoms! I *almost* oozed pus.

"*What a performance!*

"'*Get me a doctor,*' I begged. '*A doctor! A doctor!*'

"But Doctor Sarkoffagis was already informed of my arrival. He appeared now, too.

"'*I'm a doctor,*' he said.

"I felt my way toward him with my arms in the air, as if I had gone blind.

"'*A doctor!*' I continued to shout. '*Someone get me a doctor, plizz! A doctor before I die!*'

"I pounded my fists on the doctor's chest, demanding a

doctor. He continued to say he *was* a doctor. Now Miss Singh joined her voice to mine, calling for a doctor. In this way we wasted another five minutes.

"*'What seems to be the problem?'* the doctor asked me.

"Vospop, I told him every symptom for every disease from tennis elbow to leprosy. I not only told him. I *acted them out.* I acted a steetch in my side. I acted an ache in my neck. I acted a stab in my buttox. I acted a pinch in my *krotchki.*

"All this time, Meero, Nurse Damantis is looking at me fonny. She says to me:

"*'I could swear,'* she said, *'that I've met you recently. You had a mustache . . .'*

"Just then—in the distance—*pow!*

"*'What was that . . .?'* the doctor said. This *pow,* of course, was the sound of Mr. Stoodgly's peestol firing in the kitchen.

"The nurse said to Igor, *'Go see what that was.'*

"That was when I threw myself on the floor and had a magnificent fit. I had spasms like electrical eel. I foamed at the mouth like a can of shaving cream. I rolled my eyes so far into the back of my head, I could see my own brains.

"*'You must help him!'* Miss Singh sang out.

"They forgot about the peestol shot for a moment and gathered around me.

"I fit in a second fit, on top of the first! If Hollywood producer had seen me, I would be major movie star tomorrow.

"When this fit passed, the doctor again signed to Igor to go check what was the *pow.*

"I grabbed Igor's arm. I pulled him down close to me for powwow. I said:

"'You must take me! Now I am seek, but once I was voted Healthiest and Handsomest Organs in Lower Slobovia!'

"I could see that greed in their eyes, Vospop. I could feel their hunger for my organs.

"'You're a perfect candidate for Pilgrim's Paradise,' the nurse said to me—exactly as she said to your poppup, Vospop. To Igor she said, 'Take him upstairs.'

"'But wait!' I cried. 'What can you offer me at this Pilgrim's Paradise?'

"I made them show me the Technicolor brochures. I asked what kind of beds they had. I asked how good is the food. I asked how long is the swimming pool. I asked what kind of television I had in my room. I asked who was the twenty-first president of the United States. I asked what is the capital of North Dakota. I asked them to explain Einstein's theory of relativity.

"That was when Mr. Awakan Singh honked his horns outside. This was our signal that the last of the patients was out and all the trucks were gone.

"I sprang to my feets.

"'You know, I donut feel so bad now!' I said. 'Thank you for wonderful medical care. Beckwash!'

"Before they could stop us, Miss Singh and I were out the door and into Mr. Awakan Singh's taxicab.

"And so we drove away, and the curtain fell."

With flourish, my uncle took big-big bow.

"Bravo, Uncle Shpoont!" I cried. For in this way he had held the front of the Pilgrim's Paradise while we, at the back, emptied every patient from the place. We had left only the rats, the bats, the vermin, and that brown beetle paddling in the soup.

But it was only later my uncle told me all this—later, in jail. For Meero, greater and dipper trobble was yet to come. (Of course!)

Dipper and dipper,

Vospop

LADDER NINETEEN
Dobble Trobble

Dear Meero,

When the trucks returned to the illegal Slobovian section of town, the patients were taken into Slobovian homes and given seven-course meals. You would be amazed how kveekly these pipple recuperated. A slice of horseradish pie, sometimes, was all it took. But clothes had to be found, and medicines. Lockily, our Slobovian thieves and smogglers had plenty. Our Slobovian doctors and nurses, who had been working as thieves, burglars, and smogglers, spent the rest of the day tending the seek. Dood and Kyool and I went doors-to-doors again, visiting families to see that they had all they needed.

Meero, the entire illegal Slobovian section of the city was transformed. No more you saw out-of-work men and women slouching in doorways. Pipple filled the streets going from one place to another with foods and blankets. Children scampered everywhere underfeets, crisscrossing back and forth on errands. Pipple recognized me and greeted me as they passed.

I visited Erica Mannska, too. The pale, stricken, aged woman of Pilgrim's Paradise was gone. Instead I met a pretty young woman who hung on her loving husband's arm. A young woman with all her life ahead of her again.

After night had fallen, Dood said to me, "Hey, Voss man. Don't you, like, want to go home or something?"

"Or maybe like run *away*, real fast?" Kyool added. Of course he was referring to Bilias Opchuck, who was going to core me like apple at midnight.

It was by now ten o'clock p.m. We were walking up the street in front of the Stopover Café. We had been out for many hours now and were tired.

"What are you gonna do, Voss?" Kyool asked.

"You could come to my house," Dood said.

"Or my house."

"I could hide you out."

"My folks don't give a crap who I bring home, long as I don't bother 'em."

"Mine neither."

"Maybe we could scrape up some dough and, like, fly you to safety someplace. Switzerland or somethin'."

We stopped in front of my building.

"All will be well," I said. "One way or another, all will be well."

We shooked hands, rather formally.

"You're a great man, man," Kyool said.

"It's been a real honor, dood," said Dood.

Reluctantly, they left me. Both looked back at me when they went down the street. I wondered if this was the last time I would ever see them. You see, they were no longer just anuses, Meero. They were my friends.

Up in the apartment, everyone was in the kitchen, drinking *vottsdott* and celebrating. Luka Vsklzwczdztwczky was there, too, for he had also moved in. The apartment was now so crowded that Luka was going to have to sleep standing up in our broom closet.

I stared at the armchair in the living room and felt a temptation to slump into it as my father and my uncle had done in gloomy times before me. Before I could do that, Leena pulled me aside into the broom closet and shut the door for privacy.

"What is this about Bilias Opchuck meeting you at midnight?" she said.

Her eyes drilled into my brains like dobble corkscrews. To avoid her gaze, I unhooked a dustpan and studied it as if I was interested in dustpans.

"*VOSPOP,*" she said, in That Voice. When Leena Aleenska speaks to you in That Voice, there is no refusing her.

I told her everything. I told her about Stepin N. Klozdadorski's threat. I told her I must convince her to marry him someday or Bilias Opchuck would core me like apple.

"I did not want to tell you any of this," I concluded, "because I did not want you to marry Stepin N. Klozdadorski just to save me."

"I will never marry Stepin N. Klozdadorski," she said.

I said, "I did not want you to sacrifice yourself to save me."

She said, "I will not sacrifice myself for you."

"Oh," I said.

Now a gloom as big as the Rocky Mountains began to settle

over me. Perhaps in my heart of hearts I had hoped Leena would at least *offer* to sacrifice herself for me. Perhaps I had hoped she would at least *offer* to marry Stepin N. Klozdadorski so that I would not be cored like apple.

Somebody knocked on the broom closet door.

"Leena," said Grandma Aleenska's voice, "are you in there? Luka Vsklzwczdztwczky wants to make up his bed."

"Yes, Grandma! I'll be out in a minute!"

Grandma Aleenska moved off. There seemed to be nothing more to say.

"Goodbye, mostly," I said, "Leena Aleenska."

I handed her the dustpan and stepped out of the broom closet.

Everyone was still celebrating in the kitchen. I slipped out of the apartment and went up to the roof.

I sat on the edge of the roof with my feets dangling over the edge and looked out upon this great city. Illegal immigrunts of every ilk were settling down to slipp in the houses all around me, to be tormented by happy dreams. Soon I heard the first raucous Slobovian snores through open windows and the first stars began to appear, seezling in their sockets.

My brains were all aswirl, Meero. I donut even remember now what thoughts passed through my scrambling brains. I only know that somehow I was not afraid. Although Bilias Opchuck was coming for me, I felt a wonderful calm. For it seemed to me that life is nothing but *bushweck* to *beckwash* with only a leetle time in betwin. And besides, Meero. *This was America.* America would not fail me. Somehow something could still change. Things might get worse. But they would change. They had to. This is what things do.

The stars shifted and jostled overhead. Then the bells of Saint Forensica began to chime midnight.

Bong.

Bong.

Bong . . .

"So, Vospop Vsklzwczdztwczky," a voice said behind me. *"Are you ready to die?"*

I took one last look at the shining city, got to my feets, and turned around.

It was, of course, Bilias Opchuck. His illegitimate son Stepin N. Klozdadorski stood beside him. Both had peestols. (In Slobovia, I never saw a peestol, Meero. In America, I had seen peestols aplenty, all pointing and cleeking at *me!*)

Yet that wonderful calm was still upon me, Meero. I even yawned!

"He looks very calm," Stepin N. Klozdadorski said, "for someone about to die in horrible fashion."

"This is what we call the Great Stupidity," said Bilias Opchuck. "This is normal, sometimes."

Bilias Opchuck took out some butcher knives and a grindstone and began to sharpen. The Horrible was about to begin.

"Stop," said another voice.

Leena Aleenska stepped out of the shadows.

"Leena Aleenska . . . !" Stepin breathed. "May I introduce my illegitimate father, Bilias Opchuck?"

"No," she said frostily. "This is not a social occasion. Now let me understand, Stepin. You said that Vospop would die unless he convinced me to marry you someday."

"Is true," Stepin said.

"Well," she said, "Vospop has convinced me."

"*No!*" said Stepin.

"Yes," she said calmly.

"No, Leena!" I said.

"Yes, Vospop," she said. Meero, she seemed even calmer or more stupid than I was!

"So you will marry Stepin?" Bilias Opchuck asked her.

"No," she said.

"*WHAT?!*" we all cried.

Leena said, "You told Vospop that he must convince me. Vospop *has* convinced me. I am convinced that I should marry Stepin someday. You did not say I actually had to *marry* Stepin. I only had to be convinced. Well, I am convinced. But I will not marry him."

This was reedle indeed, Meero! True Slobovian logic!

"But . . ." said Stepin. "But . . . But . . . But . . . But . . . But . . ." His but's puttered out into leetle puffs of air.

"What do we do, Poppup?" Stepin finally whimpered. "She is convinced, but she still won't marry me!"

Bilias Opchuck pondered this a moment. Then he said:

"We are criminals. We have no honor. *We core him anyway!*"

Just then, a thousand sirens sounded in the streets. Red and white flowers of light burst into swirling life on the sides of all the buildings around us. As one, we ran to the edge of the roof and looked over.

The streets were filled with the twirling lights of police vehicles. Cars and vans screeched to a halt for as far as you could see. Policemen with rifles ran up the steps of every building in the street. A police captain called through a bullhorn:

"COME OUT WITH YOUR HANDS UP! THIS IS A RAID!"

The whole illegal Slobovian section of the city was surrounded.

Without a word, dropping the knives and grindstones and peestols, Bilias Opchuck and Stepin N. Klozdadorski fled into the building. I could hear them clattering down several flights of stairs. Five floors down, they ran straight into the arms of the police.

"What is all this, Vospop?" Leena asked.

In a moment I realized what was happening.

I said, "Nurse Damantis and Dr. Sarkoffagis must have gone to the police. Now the police are coming to arrest all the illegal immigrunts. This means all Slobovians and the patients from Pilgrim's Paradise, too. We will all be deported before we can speak about the unspeakable things they are doing at that place."

We could still hear the police captain with the bullhorn ordering pipple out of their houses. By now policemen hustled pipple in pajamas and nightshirts toward police vans.

A stream of news vans poured into the street. Newscasters

and reporters set up cameras and microphones and started taking peektures.

"What do we do?" Leena said.

"We donut run down those stairs the way Bilias Opchuck and Stepin N. Klozdadorski did. Come on."

We fled across the black-tar roofs of the tenements. At the end of the block, a rusty, rickety fire escape ran down past the steeply tilted roof of the Church of Saint Slobovius, Plumber, and Martyr.

We rettled down the shaking iron steps of the fire escape, loosening a flurry of rusty flakes that fluttered around our heads like autumn leaves. Our trampling steps also loosened the bolts that secured the fire escape to the bricks. The whole fire escape was about to tear itself from the wall and collapse into the alley below us.

At the place where the fire escape hung alongside the bottom of the church roof, I climbed onto the shaking rail and balanced there, wobblingly. The edge of the roof lay across a yard of empty space. Betwin us and the edge of the roof was a three-story fall.

"Leena," I said, holding out my hand, "come! We have to jump!"

I donut know why, but Leena did not doubt me. She took my hand and balanced wobblingly beside me on the rail. A yard does not sound like very far. A yard with three stories below it is very much, Meero. I counted to three, and we leaped.

The tips of our shoes caught in the rain gutter on the edge of the roof. We fell forward onto the palms of our hands, leaning against the tilt of the roof.

Safe! I thought.

Then our feets began pry the rusted rain gutter away from the roof. We sleed backward over the yawning, deezy drop. In a moment the rain gutter would fall away entirely and send us plummeting to the pavement!

"*Kveek,* Vospop!" Leena cried.

Anybody else would have been dead, mostly. As it happens, Leena Aleenska is the undefeated Church-Roof-Climbing Champion of Lower Slobovia. You remember her church-roof-climbing triumphs at the competitions on Saint Slobovius Day? With expert foot- and fingertips, she found a grip on the slates. We scaled the diagonal roof upward.

Two high, narrow, open slits formed windows in the church tower. Leena scrambled up the tower's side like a rock climber, using only her unbreakable Slobovian fingernails to hold herself. She dropped through one of those slits, then reached down and hauled me up beside her. I fell through the slit into darkness.

Remember, Meero: When you are in danger, always have a big, strong girl with you!

While the police rounded up every man, woman, and child in the illegal Slobovian section, Leena Aleenska and I hid out of sight in the church tower. We heard cries in the streets, the shouting of policemen, even an occasional shot. Then we heard a *boom!* Policemen with a battering ram were forcing open the massive oak doors in the church below us. Their voices echoed in the church as they searched amongst the pews and behind the altars.

Then we heard the police trucks carrying away their prisoners.

Then the sirens faded into the distance.

Then we heard nothing but the wind.

The police had emptied every building in the entire illegal Slobovian section. Leena Aleenska and I were the only two pipple for many blocks around.

Alone with Leena,

Vospop

LADDER TWENTY
Ghost Town

Dear Meero,

In the silence of the church tower, Leena leaned against me, trembling. Instinctively, I wrapped my arms around her and held her.

"Vospop," she said, "where can we go? What can we do?"

"Actually," I said, "I have a plan."

Leena peered into my eyes through two eenches of darkness.

"Is it an impossible plan?" she asked. "Is it mad? Is it insane?"

"Yes," I said.

"Good," she said.

I said, "We have to wait for morning."

"I knew you would come up with something," she said, and sighed as she settled back into my arms. "You are djinnius."

"What is djinnius?"

"Like Albert Einstein."

"Oh," I said. "You mean *genius*."

"Exactly," he sighed.

My Eenglish must be getting very good, Meero. Now I was correcting Leena Aleenska! Maybe in time I would use correct articles like *a, an,* and *the.* Why not? I am an djinnius!

Let me tell you something, Meero. There are many worse things you can do than huddle with your arms around a girl all night in a church tower. America was fool of new experiences, but this was one of the best. It helps, too, if the night is cool and the girl is wearing a soft, tight cashmere sweater of powder blue. It helps, too, if she is substantial girl like Leena Aleenska, who has many physical charms and also the use of her brains.

As the night went on, it was amazing how she went from merely substantial to fascinating and gorgeous, Meero! How had I never appreciated her intelligence, her humor, her wisdom, her left calf, the curve of her eyelashes, the leetle roll of fat above her heeps? And she never once during the whole night spoke of marriage. For we both knew that this would be our first and last night togather because I was engaged to marry Tiffany McBloomingdale someday, no matter what. I looked forward to a lifetime of shopping and brunching and pipple who painted turds.

A bar of sunlight woke me the next morning, wrapping my eyes like a golden blindfold. Leena Aleenska was still aslipp in my arms, purring deep in her chests like a cat in a dairy. Is true, her mouth hung open and her hair was mussed and she was snoring. Who does not snore? Whose breath does not smell like old sardines upon waking? I smelled like sardines, too!

Can I tell you something, Meero? Very gently I brushed her hair into place. This, too, I had never done before. A good start to what promised to be a miserable day!

She stirred against me and opened her eyes. For a moment she had no idea where she wasn't. She stared into my eyes dreamily and blinked a few times. She stared at me. She recognized me. She slepped my face.

"Don't get any ideas," she said.

I was in love!

A trapdoor led us down a staircase into the church. Usually at that hour the pews would hold a few churchgoers or penitents awaiting confession. Today there was only an echo from our feetsteps, saying, *Nobody, nobody, nobody.* The church doors still hung open from the police battering their way in. We walked out into the empty sunshine.

The streets were weirdily empty. Not only no pipple, but no traffic. No sounds, no movement, no sign of life for blocks around. Here and there, curtains blew in and out of open windows. This only made the street look emptier. It looked as if all life had ended. The illegal Slobovian section was a ghost town.

A dog ran up and sniffed us and wagged her spotted tail, as if asking where everybody went to.

Leena and I and the dog walked with echoing feetsteps to the Stopover Café, passing no passersby. All alone in the restaurant, we made ourselves a seven-course Slobovian breakfast and a three-course breakfast for the dog.

While we sat itting at the counter, a truck roared by, its engine startling us. The driver flung onto the sidewalk a packit of today's newspeepers. I went out and got one of each.

I laid the peepers out on the counter. Every one had a photograph of the police taking pipple away or shoving them into the backs of vans. The headline in the *Times* said, "Mass Arrests in Illegal Slobovian Section. Police Descend On Immigrants. Night Raid Empties Neighborhood." The *Tribune* said, "Clean-Up Time!" The *Telegraph* said, "Send the Slobs Back Where They Came From!"

We learned that the police were holding everyone prisoner in some old warehouses that had been turned into jails. There was a photograph of one of these jails. Faces looked out from behind the bars of steel pens. I searched each face in the photograph for my father's face, for my uncle's, for anyone I knew. They were nowhere to be seen. Of course, misery erases individuality. Look in a mirror when you're miserable sometime, Meero. See if you recognize yourself.

We were washing the dishes when a taxicab screeched to a halt out front. It was, of course, Mr. Awakan Singh and his sister. Dood and Kyool jumped out of the backseat.

"What's goin' on, Voss?"

"Is it true?"

"Your uncle is in jail?" Singh-Singh Singh said.

"Lilka's in jail?" said Dood.

"And Lilka's in jail?" said Kyool.

"They and everybody else," Leena said. She waved her hand at the ghost town around us.

"Jeez," Dood said.

"It's, like, *post-nuclear*," Kyool breathed in awe.

"Is all right," I said. "I have a plan, mostly."

"Hop in!" cried Mr. Awakan Singh.

Into his taxicab we all hopped. The dog watched us leave from the stoop of the Stopover Café, waving her tail.

"Where to?" said Mr. Singh.

I said, "To the McBloomingdale Building. As fast as you can!"

On our way,

Vospop

LADDER TWENTY-ONE
The Hummer

Dear Meero,

When we arrived at the McBloomingdale Building, the security guard would not let us in.

"Your name is not on our approved visitor list," he said.

I drew myself up to my fool height (which is not so much).

"I am the fiancé of Tiffany McBloomingdale, no matter what!" I declared. "I demand to be let in! I want to see Mr. McBloomingdale!"

I felt Leena crintch at the word *fiancé*. I had no choices but to use it.

"If you don't let me in," I added, "I will have you fired, mostly!"

The security guard dialed a telephone and spoke to someone in a low voice.

"Vospop," Leena veespered to me, "maybe I should wait outside."

"I want you here," I said firmly.

The guard turned back to us.

"All right," he said. "You can go up."

He nodded me toward the elevator bank. Not the fancy elevator bank. The regular, ordinary, mortal elevator bank.

"*She* comes with me," I said, drawing Leena to my side.

"O.K.," the guard said. "But Gandhi here and Mrs. Gandhi"—he indicated Mr. Awakan Singh and his sister—"they gotta stay here. Your two surfing buddies, too."

As Leena and I dashed for the elevator, I heard Mr. Awakan Singh giving the guard an angry lecture about Gandhi. I wish I had been there to hear it, *oh*mygodyes.

Leena and I crowded into an elevator, shoulder to shoulder with secretaries and typists and office assistants and burrocrats in suits. As we rode up, I reflected that office elevators are the steel freight containers of the burrocracy. All these millions upon millions of daily office workers—are they not migrants, too, Meero? Migrating from home to office to home again like birds in their seasons?

In his 99th floor office, Mr. McBloomingdale stood at his vast peekture window. He looked out over the city with his hands clasped behind his back like a man surveying his property. For just one second I thought of my uncle, looking out over Stoppova and tinking he owned it all. The two men stood exactly the same!

"Mr. McBloomingdale," I said.

"Well, howdy, Voss!" he said, turning around. "This here's a surprise."

The front pages of every national newspeeper were spread out on the top of his desk. The desperate faces of my fellow Slobovians stared back at me from a dozen photographs.

"So you know?" I said. "You have heard?"

He nodded grimly, looking over the newspeepers. "It's a great tragedy, Voss. But who's yer lady friend? You ain't innerduced me. And how did you two manage to escape all this?"

He nodded toward the pictures of Slobovian detainees and dropped into the throne-like bleck-leather chair behind his desk.

"Set down, set down. Take yerself a seat," he said.

"This is no time for setting, Mr. McBloomingdale," I said. "We need your help."

"Yer wish is my command, Voss. You know that."

"Indeed, sir," I said, "you told me that you *owe me one.* You said that I could call in this debt anytime. I want to call this debt in now. You have influence. You know the mayor. You know the chief of polices. Intervene for us. Get all these pipple released."

I pointed to the faces staring out of the newspeeper photographs.

"But Voss," he said, "these folks are all illegals. You gotta admit it yer own self."

"But that is not why they have been arrested!" I cried.

I told him about the Pilgrim's Paradise and how I had snicked into it to save my father. He made a hollow church stipple of his hands and rested his chin on the point of the stipple while he listened. He jumped to his feet excitedly when I had finished.

"Well, gosh dang it, Voss!" he said. "Now I see it *all.* This here police raid was payback! They wanted to hush yer mouths so's you wouldn't give away their secrets. And it was a nefarious way to get back at you fer savin' all these poor immigrants trapped at this—what did you call it?"

"Pilgrim's Paradise."

"Pilgrim's Paradise. It's a crime that's happening here, that's what it is, and I'm a-gonna help you! You and me and yer lady friend are gonna go see the mayor right now. The mayor'll spring yer family and friends. All we gotta do is explain the situation."

Mr. McBloomingdale touched a button on his desk.

"Fawn," he said to his desk, "have the Hummer brought around."

"The *Hummer?*" another voice said behind me.

Tiffany McBloomindale strode into the office.

"Howdy, Tiff!" her father boomed.

He went around his desk and wrapped his arms around her like a python and hogged her.

"Dad," she said, "how come you're calling up the Hummer? Every time you take out the Hummer, something really bad happens—"

He cut her off.

"Don't you worry 'bout a thayng, honey," he said. "Voss and his lady friend and me gotta take a little ride. We got a errand at City Hall with the mayor. Now why don't you wait right here, sweetie pie. We'll be back in two shakes."

Just then Tiffany saw the newspeepers scattered across his desk.

"What's all this?" she said. "What happened?"

Like many Americans, Tiffany did not get her news from newspeepers. She got the news from comedians on late-at-night television. She picked up one of the front pages and stared at it with wondering eyes.

"*Slobovians arrested . . .*" she read out loud.

"Why don't you catch up," her father said, "and we'll be right back. So long, hon!"

Mr. McBloomingdale grabbed his cowboy hat and hustled us out the door. I called out, "Goodbye!" as we went out, but Tiffany did not seem to hear me. She was too beezy reading the headlines. She looked very worried about something.

Mr. McBloomingdale led us down a side corridor to his private elevator. This elevator was fitted with mirrors on all sides, so that it seemed to hold a thousand of us getting smaller and smaller all the way to the horizon. Mr. McBloomingdale stood betwin us with his arms around our shoulders.

"O.K., kids, here we go!"

He pressed a button. The elevator dropped so fast, I left my stomach on the 99th floor while the rest of me plunged through empty space to the ground. I was breathless when we stopped and Leena as pale as paper.

"Quite a ride, huh," he chuckled, pressing us to himself. "I love scarin' folks like that! But hey, don't you worry 'bout a thayng now. Y'er in the home stretch."

He kept his arms tightly around our shoulders and led us down a narrow corridor. At its end, a door opened onto a concrete tunnel in a private garage. A black car hunched there, waiting for us, its engine humming. It looked like a scowling military tank. This was the Hummer. An odd car indeed for a visit to the mayor!

Two men almost as big as the Hummer stood before it, their hands clasped before their guts, the way undertakers stand. But undertakers do not usually shave their heads and wear earplugs. It did not look like iPod earplugs they were wearing.

Mr. McBloomingdale did not introduce us. The undertakers made no sign they wanted to be introduced. Without a word they opened the doors.

"Why don't you kids get in the back," Mr. McBloomingdale said to Leena and me. "I'll ride shotgun up here in front with Sergey."

Sergey . . . I thought to myself. Where had I heard that name before?

When we got in, the two undertakers got in the back with us, one on either side. Leena and I sat squizzed betwin them. It was a tight fit, with the undertakers being so muscular and Leena being so substantial. The two men did not look at us or speak to us. The man next to me had a hard bulge beneath his black jacket, but he did not adjust the bulge to keep it from poking me. And this bulge felt like a gun!

The moment the doors closed, the car shot through the concrete tunnel and almost turned over as it veered into the street alongside the McBloomingdale Building. It whipped back and forth around some cars and stopped for the light at the corner.

"There's Dood and Kyool!" I said.

They were standing out front of the building with Mr. Awakan Singh and his sister. All four were looking toward the entrance, as if expecting Leena and me to come out that way.

I moved to tap the window. My undertaker neighbor batted my hand down silently, without a look.

"Could you open window, plizz?" I said. "I want to talk to my friends."

The undertaker said nothing and kept looking out his window. He showed no sign I had spoken.

"Mr. McBloomingdale—" I began. Then I saw that the front and the back of this car were separated by a sheet of reinforced glass.

It was too late. The light changed and we zoomed away.

"Vospop," Leena said to me quietly, "this is not the way to City Hall."

I looked outside. Leena was right! We were driving in the wrong direction!

I tapped on the glass betwin us and the driver. The driver did not turn around. The glass had to be very thick for him not to hear me. I knocked and banged on the glass.

"We're going the wrong way!" I shouted.

My undertaker neighbor again batted my hand down. I said to him, "We have to tell the driver. We're going the wrong . . ."

That was when I realized where we were going. I donut

know how I knew. I felt Leena know it, too, beside me. The realization raised all the hair on the arms of her cashmere sweater.

The Hummer swerved into an alley full of broken glass and dog turds and stopped before a familiar shabby, peeling door. Two more undertakers with shaved heads and Secret Service earplugs stood waiting for us. They opened the doors of the Hummer and roughly hauled us out. As Mr. McBloomingdale got out, his celephone rang.

"Howdy, Tiff!" he boomed into it. "Yeah, we just got to City Hall this minute."

His eyes narrowed on me. He poot his hand over his celephone.

"Take 'em inside," he growled to the undertakers. Then into the celephone he said, "Naw, I don't think we'll be too long, sweetie. I don't think we'll be long a-tall . . ."

By now our undertakers had pooshed us through the peeling door into the Pilgrim's Paradise.

Hoping I see you again sometime,

Vospop

LADDER TWENTY-TWO
The Shock Chamber

Dear Meero,

Mr. Stoodgly stood waiting amidst the fleekering ruins of the repulsive Pilgrim's Paradise kitchen. The undertakers led us to him. He stared into my eyes with naked hatred. When last I had seen him, I was throwing skillets at him. Now a strip of white gauze covered his broken nose and his eyes were ringed with purple.

He speet in my face and called me an obseenity. Then he looked at Leena with up-and-down contempt.

"Take them away," he said. The undertakers pooshed us onward.

As we passed by that old cauldron of soup, I looked in. The brown beetle was floating belly-up on the greasy scum, his dead legs twisted awry like the hands of my pocket watch. Those insect legs seemed to be trying to tell me the time. They seemed to say: *It's later than you tink.*

How odd it was to see again the doors to the Employee Dining Room and the black door to the stairwell. How odd it was to be back in the shabby corridor behind the kitchen.

In the meedle of that corridor, two empty gurneys sat waiting.

Mr. McBloomingdale joined us, clapping shut his cele-

phone. To me he said, "Regards from my darlin' daughter."
To the undertakers he said: "Strap 'em down."

Leena and I stroggled, but it was no uses. We were laid
down flat and locked down with thick leather straps. With
our arms and hands trapped at our sides and even our heads
locked in place, the only way we could look was up. Like dead
pipple.

I heard the shrieking and groaning of the service elevator
as it descended. The folding steel gate rettled open. Leena and
I were wheeled into the elevator and it began to move. We
were going downwards, Meero. To the basement. To the Shock
Chamber.

One story . . .

Two stories . . .

Three stories . . .

The air grew colder and colder. When we arrived, my
breath was ghosting in the air above me like a queevering,
sheevering soul.

Then I heard another voice. A white and starchy voice.

"Welcome back, *Tom Sawyer*."

The mist of my breath turned to ice crystals. Nurse Damantis came up beside my gurney and leaned her face over mine.
She studied me with her colorless eyes. I could smell her. She
had the dry, antiseptic smell of the inside of a latex glove.

"What a treat," Nurse Damantis said. "All-natural, all-
organic Slobovian organs. And two complete sets of them.
Both young. Both in perfect health."

She looked over at Leena, then back to me.

"The two of you should fetch a pretty penny. All your *pieces* should, I mean. How odd that it's the penniless of the earth who are worth a fortune. And I can't wait to see Dr. Sarkoffa-gis take you apart. I might take a scalpel and slice out a piece or two myself, just for old times' sake. Maybe I'll slice out your Slobovian heart. I'd cut it out while you were still alive if I could. I'D *RIP* IT OUT WITH MY BARE HANDS!" she screamed into my face.

She bent so close I could feel her cold breath, like a frigid kiss.

My entire body vibrated. I strained against the leather straps in vain.

"These two won't make up for what we lost," the doctor said grimly. "They won't make up for all the patients they stole from us."

"Patients?" I said to the ceiling. "*Victims*, you mean!"

They paid me no attention.

"Don't you worry, Doc." This was Mr. Bloomingdale's voice. "We'll find a whole slew o' new patients for ya once the old batch gets deported. There ain't no shortage o' filth comin' to our American shores. We'll get 'em. We'll get 'em all and slice 'em up into mincemeat! We'll open Pilgrim's Paradise branches in every big city in this country! We'll skim the scum off the American melting pot and make enough money to buy our *own* damn country!"

He now stepped up beside the gurney I was on. He looked down at me and laid a hand on my chest, the way a man lays a hand on the hood of a car he has bought.

"It's too bad you had to step in, Voss," he said. "I liked you. I really did. And I coulda done something with you. I coulda brought you into the business and made you richer than Midas. Y'see, what you didn't know is that *I own Pilgrim's Paradise.* Why, the whole dang operation was my idea! 'Cuz this world's got a lotta rich folks lookin' fer body parts and it's got a whole lotta poor folks with the parts. The *spare* parts. That's what you people are. Y'er the spare parts o' the world, givin' yer sickly betters the wherewithal to get on with our business.

"You were right about one thayng, though," he went on. "I do know the chief o' police. I called him up first thayng when Nurse Damantis told me some Slobovian busted in and stole all our patients. I'm the one who had the chief send in the force to clean out yer stinkin' slum. But I didn't know it was you who tried to ruin me till you and yer lady friend walked into my office this mornin'.

"Well," he drawled, "my daughter's gonna be real heartbroke when you disappear off the face o' the planet. But speakin' of *heartbreak,* Tiffany's got a little problem with her ticker. Maybe I'll give her your heart instead of sellin' it to a business colleague of mine in Cairo. Ain't that true love? Exchangin' hearts with yer loved one?"

"Kill me," I said, "but not Leena."

"Sorry, pardner," he said. "Y'er goin' together. In a coupla minutes y'er gonna get to know what it's like to get so scared, yer heart just . . . *stops.* It's a ingenious invention, this here Shock Chamber. The brainchild of my good friend Dr. Sarkoffagis."

He patted the doctor's arm. "Take 'em in," he said.

The undertakers wheeled us down the corridor. I heard the groan of a heavy iron door, then found myself looking up at the lights in the Shock Chamber's soundproof ceiling.

"*Leena!*" I called out.

"I'm here, Vospop," her voice said beside me.

How I wished, Meero, that my arms were free so that I could take her hand one last time.

Time for me was about to stop like the waving, crazy hands on my ancient pocket watch. I was about to be scared to death.

Scared to death already,

Vospop

LADDER TWENTY-THREE
To The Rescue

Dear Meero,

"All right, boys and girls," Mr. McBloomingdale's voice said. "Time's a-wastin'. Let's do it!"

Just then, another voice rang out, loud and clear.

"Everybody stop right where you are."

I heard the cleek of a peestol.

It was Tiffany McBloomingdale's voice.

"Hey, Tiff!" Mr. McBloomingdale said. "What's goin' on here? What're *you* doin' here . . . ?"

"Put your hands up, everybody," she said. "*Now!* Put them *high!* You too, Daddy, or I swear to God I'll fire."

"Tiff—" his voice said.

"I said *don't move, Daddy!*"

A shot rang out, deafening in this tiny space. Mr. McBloomingdale screamed in pain. I heard him crumple to the floor with a groan.

"She shot me . . . !" he said in wonder. "My own daughter shot me . . . !"

He whimpered and moaned and swore in agony.

"Next time it won't be your knee," Tiffany's voice said. "It'll be right through the heart—if you have one. Dood. Kyool. Unstrap Voss and Leena."

Now Dood's face appeared over me, grinning, as he unhooked my straps.

"Mr. Singh," Tiffany said, "frisk the others for weapons."

Freed from our bonds, Leena and I jumped from our gurneys to see Mr. Awakan Singh freesking the doctor, the nurse, and the undertakers. Mr. Singh did it expertly, too. What we did not know was that before Mr. Awakan Singh became an American taxicab driver, he was chief of police in Upper Kashmir. (He was from Kashmir, and Leena was *in* cashmere. Is poetry to life sometimes, Meero!)

Mr. McBloomingdale moaned and writhed on the floor with a small, bloody hole in his trousers through the center of the knee. Tiffany stood in the doorway with a gold-plated peestol in her hand. She no longer looked like a brainiless teen princess, Meero. She looked like hero.

"You loved me so much you gave me everything, Daddy," Tiffany said. "You even gave me a pistol for my protection and shooting lessons so I'd be a crack shot. Thank you for that. You also gave me a phone with a GPS system so you could never lose track of me. Why do you think I called you in the Hummer? How do you think I tracked you here? How do you think I found this . . . this *prison?* And you *own* this place? You *thought* of this?"

"It—it ain't true, honey," Mr. McBloomingdale stammered. "Whatever you think, sweetie pie, it just ain't true!"

"Too bad I heard it all," she said. "We were listening in the stairwell. In fact, I *recorded* it all on this handy-dandy phone you gave me."

Mr. McBloomingdale's face sagged.

Tiffany said, "It isn't going to look pretty when the police come to arrest you and your friends and the newspapers get hold of your story."

"No," Mr. McBloomingdale groaned. "No, honey."

"Yes, honey," she said. "As soon as they get here, I'm going to take all my newspaper and magazine friends on a personal tour of this place. I think your friend the chief of police will talk up a storm."

"Maybe he'll talk," Mr. McBloomingdale said, "but the papers ain't gonna print nothin'. I *own* the dang newspapers!"

"Did you forget?" Tiffany said. "I'm the cash cow of the glossy magazines. I'm the trash they feed the public. I'm the media's darling. *They'll print whatever I do or say.* Celebrity beats money any day, Dad. Dood, Kyool—lock them in."

We backed out the door and shut Mr. McBloomingdale and the nurse and the doctor and the undertakers into total darkness. If they screamed, we did not hear them. The Shock Chamber was designed to be soundless.

Two minutes later, the police arrived and behind them the newspeepers and news channels.

You think all is well now, Meero, and we are saved? Of course not, mostly. For after they arrested Mr. McBloomingdale and his accomplices, the police arrested Leena and me and Mr. Singh and his sister as illegal immigrunts and took us away in a van.

Awaiting deportation,

Vospop

186

LADDER TWENTY-FOUR
In the Cage

Dear Meero,

The detention center where the police brought us was once a meatpacking warehouse. The steel pens where they kept the prisoners were the cages where they had kept the cattle. Every pen could hold perhaps ten cows or twenty pipple. Ours held fifty, mostly Slobovian.

In the center of each pen was a bucket for a toilet. Lockily, coming from Slobovia, many of us were used to worser toilets. It is not in any case part of the Slobovian nature to complain. Stony-faced policemen with rifles marched by the bars every minute of the day.

I ended up in the same pen with my father and my uncle and Tomas Mannsky. Naturally, my father fell upon me with shouts and tears and embracings when he saw me enter. The rest of the men in our cage were ex-patients from the Pilgrim's Paradise who had been arrested in the raid.

(How fitting that we were locked in a "pen"! I have used up so many *pens* writing you these ladders, Meero! Are not these ladders a kind of *pen* for my thoughts and memories? I have written you hundreds and thousands of sentences. Now I was to be *sentenced* myself. You see how well the world is poot together, Meero. Like Shiksepeer!)

The neighboring pen held Stepin N. Klozdadorski and his illegitimate father, Bilias Opchuck. They were not embracing. They were not talking. I reflected as I looked at them that it was love that had saved me from the Shock Chamber. If Mr. McBloomingdale had not loved his daughter, he would not have given her that peestol and the shooting lessons and the celephone that helped her find me. Mr. McBloomingdale himself was fool of hatred. But it was love for his daughter that saved me—and ruined him.

We could not leave the pen. We could have no visitors. For food we were given white cardboard boxes with a dried sandwich, a dead vegetable, and an ancient slab of cake—the same food as at the Pilgrim's Paradise. That inedible cake was Bilias Opchuck's just desserts. You should have seen him trying to swallow it!

I had been at the detention center perhaps one hours when a police captain walked up to the bars of our pen.

"Is there somebody named Vospop here?"

"I am Vospop," I said.

He motioned for another policeman to unlock the gate of the pen and for me to step out. They marched me down the long rows of pens toward a door. Faces of men, women, and children looked out at me from behind steel bars. In the last cage, I glimpsed Leena and Grandma Aleenska, but I was taken out before I had the chance to speak to them.

In a makeshift office, a red-haired man in a suit sat behind a desk reading some papers. This large room must have been where they had once slaughtered the cattle. The floor was still stained with dried brown blood.

"This is Vospop," the police captain said.

The redheaded man did not look up at me. He continued reading his papers. All I saw of him was the top of his thinning red hair and the sweat drops that beaded his scalp.

"Is this your full name?" he asked.

He thrust a printed document into my face. My name was filled in, in ink.

"Yes," I said. I did not have time to read the document. He took it away too fast.

He signed the paper, stamped it, and banged a gavel on the desk as if this were an auction.

"Deported," he said.

"I want a lawyer," I said. "Is this not America? Is this American justice?"

He merely said: *"Next."*

The policemen marched me back to my pen. When I arrived, no one needed to ask me where I had been taken. They had all been there already. They had all been marched to the red-haired man and sentenced to deportation. Now we only had to wait to be taken away.

When night came, we were too many in the cell to slipp all at once. Half the men lay down on the cold, dirty concrete. The other half stood about quietly, leaning against the bars. I heard the familiar Slobovian snores and the familiar moans of men tormented by happy dreams.

Sometime toward dawn a guard smoggled us the morning newspeepers. The front pages carried fool-page peektures of Mr. McBloomingdale and Nurse Damantis and Dr. Sarkoffagis and Mr. Stoodgly as they came in handcuffs out the golden doors of the Pilgrim's Paradise. The headline in the *Times* said: "Noah McBloomingdale Implicated in International Scheme to Sell Body Parts." The *Tribune* said: "Multibillionaire's Personal Torture Chamber!" The *Telegraph* said: "Prisoner's Paradise!" There were also many peektures of the squalid rooms and hellish halls and the putrid kitchen at Pilgrim's Paradise.

These newspeepers were passed from hand to hand and pen to pen. They were handled until they nearly shredded into rags. Even the policemen wanted to read them. And when the policemen had read, they no longer shouted at us so. Indeed, they looked upon us with very different eyes.

"It ain't right," I heard one policeman mutter as he read.

At nine o'clock we heard many loud engines outside. The police captain came down the aisle, shouting, *"All out! All out!"*

One by one the cages were unlocked and we were marched into a parking lot. Dozens of yellow school buses with armed guards sat lined up to take us away. Some pipple cried out at the sight of the buses. Most who cried were the former patients of Pilgrim's Paradise, for their relatives still did not know where they were. Now they would disappear a second time. And to where, Meero? Where would we all be sent?

As I was getting onto my bus, I glimpsed Leena getting onto another, farther down the line. She turned and looked around as if searching for someone. I called her name, but she did not see me. Who knew when and where Leena Aleenska and I would ever meet again?

The police captain blew a whistle and waved his arm for the first bus to head out. Before the bus could move, a sergeant ran up to the captain and said something in his ear. The captain halted the bus. The two talked for a moment. The captain went to the driver of the lead bus and said something to him through the side window. Then he blew his whistle and waved us all to go. The lead bus roared out of the parking lot. The other buses followed.

I sat next to my father. My Uncle Shpoont sat behind us. All of us looked out the school bus windows at the passing city, and everything we looked at looked like a memory. The present already felt like the past. For we were to lose everything that we were seeing. How funny, Meero, that we should be traveling in school buses! As if we had been turned into children again—children on their way to a very deefeecold lesson.

Ah, well, I thought, expecting to see the highway any second. *The next chapter in my adventure begins.*

"Vospop," my father said to me in a low voice, "this is not the way out of town."

My next chapter had begun sooner than I am thinking.

Heading the wrong way,

Vospop

LADDER TWENTY-FIVE
Bushweck, America!

Dear Meero,

My father was right. We were not heading toward the highway, but toward the meedle of the city! Policemen lined our route now, stopping traffic to let us go by. Imagine our surprises when the buses halted, one after another, in the vast space before the steps of City Hall. And imagine to yourself, Meero, that a great crowd of pipple filled the building's broad stone steps already!

News vans surrounded City Hall, filming us as we descended from the buses. Flashbulbs went off like firecrackers. Spectators held up celephones to record us and send us to their friends. Veedeo cameras rolled in a hundred hands as a police escort led us up the steps and arranged us in rows. Were we to be publicly humiliated before deportation? Were we perhaps to be publicly *executed*?

The police captain approached me and my uncle and said, very gravely, "Follow me."

The crowd parted before us as the captain led us up farther. I expected to see a gallows or a guillotine at the top of the steps. Instead I saw a podium draped in red, white, and blue and a woman who looked familiar somehow, coming down to meet me with her hand out, as if to shake mine . . .

"Vospop?" she said. "I'm Mayor Doris X. Machina."

The mayor of the city, Meero! And she was now drawing me and my uncle alongside her at the podium! Was I to kneel? Salute? Kiss her hand? And what do you call a mayor? Your Highness? Your Majesty?

"Call me Doris," she said. Then she stepped up to the microphone and her voice boomed and echoed around City Hall Square.

"Ladies and gentlemen," she announced. "Today I am proud to bring to you a hero of our city. I bring you Vospop Vsklzwczdztwczky!"

The crowd shouted "HOORAY!"

The cheering almost deafened me. Even the policemen were cheering, Meero! And also the pipple hanging out the windows of skyscrappers all around the city square! That was when I saw Tiffany McBloomingdale standing at the bottom of the steps. I hardly recognized her, for she was dressed in a long, black woolly garment—very plain, almost drab. She looked like nun.

It took the mayor five minutes to calm everyone down so that she could speak again.

"I'm sure you've all read today's newspapers," she said into the microphone. "I'm sure you've read with horror about what a group of innocent people had to go through. I'm sure you've read with endless admiration about the bravery of some dedicated patriots. That's right, I say patriots!"

After another cheer, the biggest one yet, the mayor went on.

"The criminals responsible for these acts have been arrested. They will be prosecuted to the full extent of the law. I have in my hand a signed deportation order for Vospop Vsklzwczdztwczky . . ."

A great "BOO!" went around the crowd.

She went on. "I also have deportation orders for all his compatriots and the people they saved!"

An even louder "BOO!"

"These people are being deported as illegal immigrants. I see only one recourse," Mayor Machina said. "Vospop, would you please raise your right hand? Would you *all* please raise your right hand?"

A thousand solemn right hands rose, including my own. And there, Meero, on the steps of City Hall, Mayor Doris X. Machina swore us in as citizens of the United States of America. When she had finished, she said:

"As mayor of this great city, I hereby present to Vospop Vsklzwczdztwczky this city's highest award, the medal of honor."

She pinned a great weight of silver to my bazoom. I could hardly see it, Meero, for a flood of tears blurred everything around me! What I *could* see was my father, the undefeated Tree-Throwing Champion of Lower Slobovia, throwing up his hands in helpless joy. He had to throw *something*.

The mayor said, "I am also proud to present to Mr. Shpoont, for *his* contribution to this heroic rescue, the key to our city."

The mayor handed my uncle an enormous gold key. Uncle

Shpoont held the key reverently in his hands, like baby. The glow from the gold plating glinted in his eyes.

"Vospop," he said, "I thought I owned this city. Guess what? *I DO OWN THIS CITY!*"

Mayor Machina returned to the microphone.

"Let me also mention Mr. Awakan Singh, cab number CO1935, and his sister, Miss Singh-Singh Singh. In addition, the city wants to thank Zack Willis and Shawn Jackson for their contribution."

I heard a raucous cheer nearby. I saw Dood and Kyool pumping their fists in the air and five-highing each other.

"Dood!"

"Kyool!"

"Ohmygodyes!" cried Mr. Awakan Singh.

The mayor took out a paper and said: "I hereby declare that this date will henceforth be known in our city as Slobovian Day!"

Another deafening cheer. The mayor shooked my hand one last time.

"Welcome to America," she said to me. "You're free now, Vospop."

"Plizz!" I said. "Call me Voss!"

In this moment, a newspeeper person thrust a camera into my face and said, *"Smile, kid!"*

A flash blinded me and left stars and stripes flashing before my eyes, not to mention rockets' red glare.

Now everyone in the square was yelling and embracing and shaking hands. Policemen and total strentchers patted me on the back. A woman gripped my arm and said, "I'm going to name my child Vospop, after you!"

I descended the City Hall steps to the curb, where Tiffany stood.

"I did not have the chance to thank you for saving us," I said to her. "But I will have many chances after we are married someday, no matter what."

"No, Voss," she said. "We can't be married. You see, I'm going into a convent to take vows of poverty and chastity. I'm going to dedicate my life to good works. So I release you from your promise of marriage. It was, like, real nice of you to offer."

No wonder she looked like nun, Meero. She *was* a nun! Sister Tiffany!

She threw her arms around my neck and held me for a moment, then got into a waiting car. She looked out the window at me and weegled her fingers goodbye. Then she set her leeps to the window and left a misty kiss there. The imprint of her leeps on the glass looked like a broken heart.

Watching her ride away,

Vospop

LADDER TWENTY-SIX
The Red-Eyed Hero of New Slobovia

Dear Meero,

The Slobovian section of the city went crazy that night. I should say the *legal* Slobovian section went crazy, for we were illegal no longer. A traditional Slobovian band (piano, accordion, tuba, kazoo, and bagpipe) set up in front of the Stopover Café, with Luka on piano. For many avenues all around there was nothing but dancing and singing American citizens from street to shining street! Not only Slobovians, but all the former prisoners of the Pilgrim's Paradise were there with their families. The street was like a map of the world, Meero!

The Stopover Café was hopping with beeznest. Not only packed with customers, but five extra waitresses! The owner of the café, in honor of Slobovian Day, had forgiven the back rent and extended the lease for one hundred years. So the restaurant was saved after all!

The first thing I had done, Meero, upon coming back to the apartment that day? I had thrown the Armchair of Gloom out the window. It landed on the sidewalk, upside down. Children were playing cowboys and Indians on it now.

Standing on the steps of our building, I looked down into the crowd and saw my father dancing the Sloboviana, kicking his legs higher than anyone around him.

"Vospop!" he called to me. "Come dance!"

Next to my father, Uncle Shpoont danced with Singh-Singh Singh. He shouted to me:

"How do you like my street, Vospop?"

"I like it, Uncle!" I shouted back. "I like it very much!"

I saw Erica and Tomas Mannsky dancing, too. I saw Dood dancing with Lilka and Kyool dancing with Lilka. Dood and Kyool were wearing gray fedora hats. They waved their gray fedora hats at me and shouted, *Bushweck,* Vospop!"

Pipple passing by shooked my hands and patted my shoulder. Somebody had started calling me "the red-eyed hero of New Slobovia." Now everybody was calling me that.

My answer was always the same. "I cannot be this hero. I donut have red eyes."

Leena Aleenska moved up beside me on the steps. Togather we looked over the crowd.

She said, "I have news for you, Voss."

This is first time ever she called me "Voss"!

She handed me the evening newspeepers. My peekture filled all the front pages. The headline in the *Times* next to my photograph said: "Voss *Populi.*" The *Tribune* said: "Voss Is Boss!" The *Telegraph* said, seemply: "Hero."

The peekture on all these front pages was the photograph taken at the end of the ceremony at City Hall. The funny thing was, Meero: The camera flash had turned my eyes *red.*

"An accident," I said to Leena. "A coincidence."

"No," said Leena. *"Fate."*

"Speaking of fate," I said, "Stepin N. Klozdadorski and

Bilias Opchuck have released us. You donut have to marry Stepin someday, and I will not be cored like apple. They even provided the imitation blackmarket Chiss Poffs for tonight's festival. You see? They are true Slobovians after all."

Leena hooked her arm into mine and sighed. She was wearing again the soft, tight cashmere sweater of heavenly powder blue. I knew that we were both tinking of the night we spent togather in the church stipple. From old instinct at such moments, I took out our ancient family pocket watch to find the time. That was when I noticed a most curious thing, Meero.

The watch had started running again.

The glass was still shattered. The hands were still crazy. But the hands were *moving,* Meero. I held the watch to my ear. *Teek tok, teek tok* like a healthy Slobovian heart.

"So, Voss," Leena Aleenska said to me. "Do you tink we will marry someday, no matter what?"

"Time will tell," I said, "mostly."

And we danced the Sloboviana all night.

Come over to America, Meero. Is *good.*

Red-white-and-blue-eyed,

Voss

LADDER TWENTY-SEVEN
Aboard Sheep

Bushweck, Voss!
George Clooney and I are now in meedle of Atlantical Ocean. George is not so happy, mostly, for we are locked in blackmarket imitation Porta Potti. Is not much room in Porta Potties for growing Slobovian boy and fool-grown cow. As you Americans say, we make do.

We will be seeing you soon. So save me, plizz, a slice of horseradish pie. And save one for George, too. She says, Moo.

Your eternal and approaching friend,

Meero